M000295186

The Suitor's Treasure

David DeVowe

His Visible Hand Books

See God's hand in _your_ life.

DEDICATION

To all those in search of the Treasure.

For the invisible things of him from the creation of the world are clearly seen...
–Romans 1:20

Contents

ACKNOWLEDGMENTS

Cover design: Michael DeVowe Creative Works
Cover illustration: Hannah Firezar

1

Home Again, Home Again

Every *other* trip to Maple Hill held as much excitement as lutfisk. Who would have known the little town harbored a secret nearly as heart-stopping as the discovery of a dead body in Stoney Creek's hot pond?

The summer of 1924 had barely passed. You would think that the arrest of the Hawthornes and the shooting of Sarge Malvern would have been enough excitement for a whole lifetime—especially for a boy who'd just turned twelve.

But ever since MaryAnne DuPree busted into Stoney Creek, nothing had been the same. If it weren't for her, I would have never stepped foot in Grandma's attic. And because of that, we were bound together on a search for something no one else thought to be true.

I was hopeful. But MaryAnne *believed*.

***

The best seat left in the wagon was the heavy, folded tarp underneath me. Wet, cold air nipped my face as I held my choppers up over my scarf. I was glad Mama made me wear a scarf. The days had been bitterly cold—and drier than any November I knew. Now the wind began to blow strongly from the south, promising warmer weather.

"Good traveling weather for Thanksgiving," Dad said from the driver's seat.

I suppose that was true, seeing how most Novembers were covered in snow. Dad took us to Grandma and Grandpa's whenever Thanksgiving roads were passable. It was warm last year when the Johnsons lent us their surrey. But things had shaped up quite differently this time.

For one, Dad borrowed a lumber wagon from the mill for our trip. He got promoted from stacking lumber to driving a team, and Dad said the wagon was one of his perks. Whatever that was, it didn't feel so good. Johnson's surrey was too small for the seven of us anyway, and the DuPrees didn't have transportation of their own.

"Are you doing okay, Margaret?" Mrs. DuPree asked Mama with a look of concern.

"I'm fine," Mama said. "I'm doing just fine." Ladies fussed like that when a baby was comin'. Just about the time school started, Dad told me and Ricky over supper that our family was going to change.

"Shoe, Ricky—you're going to have a new brother or sister soon."

"Tomorrow?!" Ricky kneeled on his chair and bounced up and down.

I smirked. Mama didn't look like she would have a baby, at least not tomorrow.

"No, not tomorrow, Ricky," Dad smiled.

"When?!" Ricky yelled.

"February. Sometime in February, Ricky. That's after Christmas." Dad had grinned across at Mama and Mama smiled back.

So when Mrs. DuPree inquired if Mama was okay, that's how I knew she asked about more than just Mama as we jostled down the State Road. Dad drove while Mr. DuPree sat on the driver's seat beside him. The rest of us were in the bed. Dad had fashioned seats for the moms out of sacks and hay. Ricky laid down with his head on Mama's leg while I sat on my hard tarp with Oscar's chin on my knee.

MaryAnne giggled, "I haven't seen your nosth that red since the first time we walked to school together, Shoesth."

I smirked with my eyes since that's all I had for her, on account of my scarf.

MaryAnne had started sixth grade with the same lisp she had in the fifth. Her lisp didn't show up nearly as much anymore, but it never missed my name. I had failed to stop her from calling me Shoes last winter, and I had given up on her tongue-pronunciation of a name as simple as any nickname a UPer could own.

It was a nice change—if change could be nice—to have someone besides Ricky along on the ride. But after two hours of getting knocked around on a lumber wagon, the novelty had worn off. MaryAnne responded to my smirk by raising an eyebrow at me, then smiling upside down.

Funny how she did that—an expression for which I had no response. It wasn't a frown. It would have been a perfect smile if I could stand her on her head. But I couldn't do that. Mama would throw a fit if I treated a girl that way.

MaryAnne pressed into her mama until the two were likely to tip over. They were an unmatched pair. Except for the smiles, MaryAnne didn't look much like her ma. Mrs. DuPree's wavy, blonde hair fell out of her winter wool church hat on every side. I called it a church hat 'cause no one else wore a hat like that except for Sunday. Her eyebrows were as soft as the rest of her face, so as hardly to be seen.

Next to her, MaryAnne's hair appeared redder and darker than usual. Dark eyebrows for a redhead, too, with a sprinkling of freckles across the high part of her cheeks— nothing like her ma. Made me wonder where she got all that—until she caught me looking. That was embarrassing. I didn't want her gettin' any wrong ideas.

"Staying warm, sweetie?" said Mrs. DuPree, squeezing her daughter hard enough to force one of MaryAnne's eyes closed.

"My toes are cold."

"Wiggle them, honey. It'll help keep you warm." Mrs. DuPree pulled their blanket up further under MaryAnne's chin.

Mama had insisted that she invite the DuPrees for Thanksgiving since they didn't have family of their own to visit. Dad didn't know how to get us all there, and he wasn't so sure about dropping in on Mama's parents with another bunch.

"Margaret, your folks won't take kindly to strangers spending the night," Dad had said.

"The DuPrees are not strangers, Toivo. Besides, I'll write Ma a letter so she'll know to expect more of us this year." Mama was quite capable of reasoning possibility when she wanted her way. Dad finally gave in to Mama when he devised his transport plan.

That's how five of us ended up in the back of a lumber wagon. Every now and then Dad broke the awkward silence up front.

"How's the new job, Adrien?" Dad asked. Mr. DuPree hadn't received another investigation appointment since the Hawthorne's case closed, so he had taken a job loading logs on the rail spurs.

"Glad to have work," replied Mr. DuPree. "God is good to provide between assignments." There was a long pause. That's how our dads did it—not like the ladies. Mr. Dupree continued, "God has given us new friends, too. You and Margaret and the boys have been a real blessing."

Dad grunted something that sounded as uncomfortable as I was.

"We really appreciate spending Thanksgiving with your in-laws," continued Mr. DuPree. "You're sure they won't mind?"

"Margaret wrote a letter. It'll be fine."

***

"We're there! We're there!" Ricky jumped three times before he fell off the wagon. He thrashed on the ground, both hands on one knee screaming loud enough to make it from here to town. Grandma and Grandpa lived a 10-minute ride from town. Just because Ricky screamed loud enough for folks in Maple Hill, it was no indication of the severity of his affliction. The DuPrees were all over Ricky before any of us could say, "He's probably fine."

"O-o-oh are you okay, honey?" Mrs. DuPree whined.

Ricky leveraged sympathy into a cacophony. MaryAnne was already off the wagon, casting me a look to drive conviction to the bone.

"Your little brother, Shoesth! He's hurt!"

"He does this all the time," I said. "He's probably fine." MaryAnne glared at me, horrified.

Turns out Ricky *was* fine. Not fine enough, though, to stop wailing, raising an alarm right into the house. You could see heat from the kitchen escaping over Grandpa's head as he held the front door open. We all made our way to the porch, injured display in tow.

"Well, we thought you'd never get here!" exclaimed Grandpa, stepping onto the porch. He slapped Dad on the back then gave Mama a hug. Grandpa introduced himself to the DuPrees, then turned to me. "You wanna fight?" he said, holding both fists below his chin. That was Grandpa's trademark greeting to me and Ricky—always wanting a fight.

I shook my head and smiled.

Grandpa turned on Ricky. "How about you, little whippersnapper? Ya' wanna fight?"

Ricky pawed at Grandpa, frowned deeper, and then forced out one last tear. Grandpa dropped his guard.

"Come on in before Old Man Winter blows all of us off the porch!" He held the door open while we made our way inside. I got in the door just behind Dad.

"Hello, Toivo," said Grandma.

"Hi, Ma. Good to see you!" Dad called Mama's mama Ma when Grandma wasn't his mama. That had confused me since I was born. I didn't try to explain it to MaryAnne because the look on Grandma's face just then would have halted a charging she-bear with cubs.

Grandma forced a smile onto her thin lips, but it wasn't taking. She steeled at Mama, glanced over at the DuPrees, then bore down on Mama again.

"You got my letter, didn't you, Ma?" asked Mama.

"Brev? Vad post brev?!" Grandma fired off words I didn't know. Perhaps she didn't want the DuPrees to know, either. "Margareta! Du vet bättre än att överraska din mamma så här?!" Grandma shot more Swedish at Mama as she pressed her apron down on all sides.

Grandma's new language wasn't covering up that she hadn't received the letter. It wasn't hiding the fact that she wasn't happy about strangers in her house, either.

I assessed the situation, planning an escape. Ricky still hung on Mama's hand, nursing for sympathy. MaryAnne got brave enough to stop studying the floor. I signaled to her with my finger to follow me down the hall. We slipped quietly to the end of the narrow passage where steep stairs led to the rooms above.

We scrambled up on all fours like the wind. Attic heat pressed on us so we dumped coats on a bed and our boots beside.

"Hey, neat," MaryAnne said as she leaned over a writing table to peer out the small window on one end of the space. "I could reach those branches from here." Frozen tips of the big oak swayed heavily just in front of the glass.

"Glad it wasn't that windy on our ride," I said.

"Who's the writer?" MaryAnne asked, shaking a pencil my way.

"Nobody, I know of," I said, turning to the inside of the room. "This is where my mom used to sleep." I walked down the center of two rooms that were separated by a curtain. The space was shaped like an *A*, allowing for a tall guy like me to stand straight up in the middle. The first room had one bed on each side, pushed against a low wall. The second room had a small window just like the first, and one big bed with a Singer treadle alongside, tucked down into its cabinet, same as always. The white wall opposite the bed was the tallest, with a door in the middle about the height of my chest. Its rusty latch was closed with an open padlock.

"What's in there?" MaryAnne asked.

"Grandma calls it her spare room. We're not supposed to go in there 'cause my mom said we could fall through." Falling through was enough to keep Ricky away from the door when we slept up there. And darkness inside the attic was mystery enough for me—when I was little.

"But what's in it?" MaryAnne persisted.

"Boxes and things. It's hard to see. I've never really looked 'cause I don't want to fall through."

"You really think you'd fall through?" MaryAnne wrinkled her forehead.

"Maybe."

"Shoe? MaryAnne?" Big-people voices seeped through the floor register by the window.

"Sounds like they noticed we were gone," I said. "We'd better get downstairs."

***

There was enough food to feed two more families when supper was over. Grandma had returned to speaking English again, but the conversation was halted, at best. Mrs. DuPree and MaryAnne did what they could to offer up help in the kitchen after supper while the men sat in the front room. The front room was the room on the side of the house with a door nobody opened, to steps that led out to the woods.

"Looks like it would be best if we didn't stay the night," said Dad to the worn, wooden floor. Grandpa leaned forward to inspect the floor too.

"She'll come around, Adrien." He looked sideways at Dad. "I keep praying for her," Grandpa said, almost to himself. "Been since the Lord changed me—and I ain't gonna stop. She'll come around—you'll see." Dad didn't know what to do with that.

"It would be best if we made our way home," he said.

Grandpa sat upright. "Sure you want to travel this late, Adrien?"

"It'll be fine." Dad got up and left the room.

Within the hour, the horses were out of the barn and hitched. Our overnight bags were loaded back into the wagon as shadows grew tall over fresh snow. The sun never did like winter in the UP. Wind had blown in a warm relief for traveling and we were full of food, but that didn't lighten the mood. Everyone dispensed halted good-byes, then we loaded up and turned onto the State Road for home. Just before trees overtook us, Ricky and I waved at Grandpa and said good-bye to the shortest Thanksgiving on record.

2

Stranded

Nobody said anything the first hour. Mr. DuPree finally broke the silence. "I feel bad that we upset your in-laws, Toivo."

"Wasn't your fault. Water under the bridge," Dad said under his breath. Then with a tone of determination, "We need to get home before this weather gets worse." Dad slapped the reins on the horses' rumps.

Heavy wet snow had begun to fall shortly after we left Grandma and Grandpa's. I scraped some off the wagon, packed it with my choppers, and then tossed it at MaryAnne, hitting her shoulder.

MaryAnne pursed her lips and narrowed her eyes as she gathered snow of her own. She threw hard, narrowly missing my face. Soon Ricky got involved and Oscar barked. All at once a strong gust of wind knocked heavy snow off of a tamarack overhead and nearly pitched Ricky off the wagon.

"Kids! Sit down," Mama said. "We don't need another mishap." She glanced up over the treetops. "I don't like the looks of this. The weather isn't letting up and I'm afraid we won't be able to get home."

Mrs. DuPree looked at Mama with equal concern. The sun had long been hidden behind clouds, and darkness closed in faster than a normal November eve.

"Toivo, don't you think we should turn around?" Mama asked Dad.

"We're about halfway." Dad seemed to be considering his options out loud. "Though we might do better turning back out of this storm."

Dad found a wide place in the road to get the team swung back toward Maple Hill. By then the wagon wheel's tracks were deep enough for snow to fall back in them as we passed. The wind took on a new chill as flakes whipped in every direction.

Dad urged the horses on. Still, they slowed ever more. Finally, Mr. DuPree got out front, pulled one of the bridles and walked the team forward as Dad drove.

Snowballs had long left my thoughts. Instead, my mind was filled with the heavy squeak of wagon wheels as they panked snow underneath. The sound would stop, and Dad would urge the team ahead. Each time we moved forward, the squeaking pank of snow grew shorter until the team could move no more. All of us in the bed huddled under a cover of darkness against the wagon's sideboards.

At the final halt Dad said, "Shoe, come here. Take my knife into the cedars there next to the road. Cut two poles about four feet long and see if you can find a couple heavier logs to hold the tarp in place."

I grabbed Dad's knife and moved toward the woods. Snow stung my eyes as I held them wide to let in a faint bit of light.

"Arthur!" Dad yelled over the wind, calling me back to the wagon. "If I can light the lantern, Mr. DuPree and I are going to unhitch the horses, then lead them back down the road to Grandpa's. You need to take care of Ricky and the womenfolk. Understand?"

I nodded my head at the dark outline of Dad's face.

"After you cut poles, fashion a tent on the wagon with the tarp. Prop it up strong. Stay close to one another to keep warm. We'll be back with help as soon as we can."

Dad rubbed my head, pushing my hat down over my eyes.

"I'm countin' on ya, son."

I bumped my hat up, then moved back toward the woods. Feeling my way around the cedars, I located two young, sturdy trees that were straight enough to prop up the tarp. After notching, I snapped them off to the right length, then cut every branch. Satisfied with my new tent poles, I kicked through the snow until I found a small, dead log, heavy enough to hold down one side of the tarp. I knew I needed a couple more. Fumbling through the darkness, I worked my way deeper into the thicket. I dragged the second log back to where the first one lay. The third was

- 19 -

harder to find. It was difficult to make out the shape of a tree against the snow. Wind howled almost steady as I turned one way, then the other, using my boots to find what I needed. Finally, I located a heavier stick that would have to do.

Turning back, I wasn't sure which direction the wagon was. I squinted at the trees around me, straining to make out a path back to the road. The more I looked, the more confused I got. I started grasping at branches, searching for direction, until my heart raced to the top of my chest.

I had to subdue panic and think. How would I find the wagon in the dark of night?

I whistled. It was the whistle Oscar held dear—the loudest whistle I could muster to pierce the storm's fury. Staying put, I whistled again.

Suddenly, a shape startled me as it burst forth from the thicket. It was Oscar, wagging his tail wildly, whimpering with delight to have found me.

I instinctively grabbed onto his collar as he dragged me and my branch back through the brush to where I laid the first two logs. It was there that I first heard Mama.

"Shoe? Arthur? Are you there, Arthur?"

I could hear worry welling up in her voice.

"Yes, Ma!" I yelled. "I'm here!"

Setting up the tent went easier than I thought. But then anything after a dark scare in a cedar swamp with a howling wind seemed easy. I was able to wedge the two poles in large cracks between wooden planks on either end of the wagon bed. We worked together to get the tarp on top and the logs to hold it down against the wind. When all was done, we had ourselves an extended teepee. At least that's how I imagined it, since there was not much to see.

After scraping the snow off the floor, we all sat in a tight circle and waited. Our tent kept the wind out but didn't do much more for keeping a guy warm. Or a girl, I suppose.

"Mama, I'm cold," MaryAnne whispered.

I heard Ricky whimpering between sniffles.

"I got ya, Ricky," Mama said. "We'll be okay. Papa's going to get help."

Help wasn't coming anytime soon, near as I could tell. I thought about what Dad had told me—take care of Ricky and the womenfolk.

"Why don't we pray?" said Mrs. DuPree.

I didn't see how it could hurt. Besides, I didn't know what else to do to take care of the womenfolk. I closed my eyes.

"Dear Father in Heaven, we come before you to plead for help in time of need. Please keep us warm tonight, let us not fear in the midst of the storm, and please, please protect our men as they go for help. Amen."

MaryAnne whispered, "Amen."

Opening my eyes didn't make any difference. It was just as dark as if I had them shut. Since Mrs. DuPree's prayer made it sound like she planned on spending the whole night, I figured we ought to save all the heat we had.

"Let's spread hay out on the floor, then put the sacks on top. If we lie down close to each other with the blankets over us, we'll stay warmer that way."

There was no response. I fumbled for the straw seats Dad had fashioned and spread it out in the center of our tent. The flour sacks went on top. I laid down in the middle over someone's feet, hoping the others would follow.

Mama put Ricky at my left. He sniffled in my ear. Then Mama laid down next to him. She began to spread her blanket over the three of us when a wet braid fell across my eyes.

"Good idea," MaryAnne whispered as I threw her braid back at her.

People squished in tighter from both sides until I was sure I wasn't going to die from hypothermia. Maybe suffocation.

Another whisper passed the short space from her mouth to my ear, "God will help us, Shoesth. You'll see."

I wondered about that.

And then, "Thanks for the tent."

***

There was a lot of breath under there when I woke. Pulling the blanket back, I sucked in thick air that chilled my lungs. A dim light poked through the opening in the tarp at the back of the wagon. *Had I slept that long?*

The tarp still whipped in the wind, but less strongly than the night before. I wondered about the others.

"MaryAnne!" I whispered out loud.

"What?"

Then Mom spoke from under the blanket, "Shoe, look outside to see if it's still snowing."

I got up, stuck my head out, and squinted at snow that looked deeper than my knees. Flakes were still falling nearly as heavily as last night. I opened the bottom of the tarp and pushed Oscar off the edge. Only Oscar's head and tail floated above the snow. He bounded twice, then stood still again.

Everyone was sitting up when I ducked back in. "The snow looks deep," I said. "I think we should leave for Grandma and Grandpa's.

"But, Shoe," Mama said between shivers, "if the snow is too deep, we'll be stranded far from here with no shelter for the night."

"I know, Ma," I said. "But we can't wait here another day, we'll freeze. Walking will keep us warm." I folded a blanket to get everyone moving. "I'll break trail. When I'm tired, we can trade off." Nobody resisted, and I figured it was our only hope. "If we start walking now, we could make it while there's still light."

I led the way with the moms and MaryAnne single file behind. Then Ricky followed with Oscar, bringing up the rear. The two of them had a pretty good path by the time the rest of us packed it down.

I made it to the first bend in the road before I got winded.

"Whew!" I said. "I need to switch."

Mama was next, but Mrs. DuPree insisted, "Let me go ahead, Margaret. A woman in your condition shouldn't be exerting yourself like that."

That's how the morning went, me, then Mrs. DuPree, then MaryAnne taking the lead. MaryAnne hadn't grown as much as me last summer, which made it difficult for her to break trail. Each time we switched off, the leader blazed a shorter distance than the last time.

By afternoon our energy had waned and turkey on my stomach had worn thin. We rested until snow in our mouths chilled our insides and sweat in our coats chilled the outside. Before starting up after one break I looked at Mama, who had fallen to the rear with Ricky.

"Mama, are you okay?" I asked. Mama's face was whiter than it should be that early in winter. She turned her head and vomited in the snow. It was the third time that day.

I looked at Mrs. DuPree, in lead position. Her face was stricken like Mama's. Dad's words came back to me, *"Take care of Ricky and the womenfolk."*

We had to press on. Taking over the lead, I high-stepped one, two, three, then paused; one, two, three, then paused. Three sets of three, then I sat again to rest. Wind and snow whipped in front of me, as strong as it had been all day. My eyebrows were frozen masses of ice, probably bigger than Grandpa's.

A brief rest, then we trudged forward again until I took only two steps before collapsing into the snow. My throat ached for water. The more snow I ate, the faster I came to the chills. Either the clouds had amassed greater than before or the sun was slipping low. We were running short on light.

With my hat on the snow, I stared up at a million flakes coming down at once. *"Take care of Ricky and the womenfolk"* kept ringing through my head.

Suddenly, a faint voice came over the wind, "Yeah! Yeah!"

I looked up, wondering if I was hearing things.

Then a little louder, "C'mon, Tater, you can do it, big boy."

"It's Grandpa!" I said.

Mama threw her head back. "Oh, good Lord."

Tater was Grandpa's plow horse. Grandpa named him that because he wanted his horse to be good at plowing a field for his favorite crop. Large billows of steam could be seen blowing from the horse's nostrils. I whistled the loudest shrill I could muster.

Dad whistled back.

Energy surged from deep inside me as I bounded forward. "Dad, you made it!" I said as I greeted him.

"Glad to see you, son." Dad wrapped one arm around me as the horse and sleigh continued ahead. Grandpa had hitched his deep powder sleigh to Tater, the one with wide skids for floating on the snow. After Grandpa managed to turn it around on the narrow road, we all loaded up. The sled didn't float on the snow a bit, but Tater had cut a good path, making it easier for our return.

Inside the sleigh were dry blankets and cold biscuits Grandma had sent for the journey. Grandpa gave two of the biscuits to Tater, got up on the driver's seat and turned back to us. "It's a good thing the bunch of you made it as far as you did. You cut a couple miles off our trip. Saves ol' Tater for getting us home." Dad held Mama close as the horse trudged our sled through deep snow.

MaryAnne smacked the front of my jacket with the back of her snowy mitten. "I told ya, Shoesth."

"Told me what?"

"That God would help us. See—we'll be back to your grandma's soon," MaryAnne said with her dimpled grin.

"Maybe we just needed to hoof it through the snow," I said.

Or maybe MaryAnne was right. One thing was for sure—never had I looked forward to seeing Grandma as much as I did that night.

3

Secret in the Attic

Warm covers never felt so good. I snuggled into one of the twin beds in the first room, Ricky in the bed opposite. Ricky was sleeping even before Dad tucked him in. Dad and Mama slept in the small room downstairs. MaryAnne and her parents quickly went quiet in the big bed across the curtain. Mr. DuPree snored while I thought on what happened that day.

I wondered why MaryAnne gave God the credit for getting us back here. Was it him that helped us, or did we simply help ourselves? I wondered how we would be doing if we had stayed with the wagon. Snow hadn't stopped all day. I supposed that our tarp tent would have collapsed under its weight. The weight of warm covers across my chest was the last I remember before falling asleep.

***

"Morning, Arthur." Grandma wasn't like Mama for morning words. She hadn't even looked at me. Instead, Grandma lifted a piece of the stove top with a wire handle to poke two pieces of wood into it.

"Morning," I said.

"Hope you're hungry."

"Hungry, all right! I could eat a horse."

"We don't have none of them for eatin'," said Grandma. "Bacon and eggs are what's cooking."

"Sounds real good to me." Something Mama taught me a long time ago was not to complain about what's to eat. Especially when we're out. Anything would have sounded good, besides.

"Your friends awake?" Grandma said as she laid strips of bacon to sizzle on a skillet.

"I dunno. Didn't sound like it when I came down." Just then I heard the stairs squeak under somebody's load.

"Good morning, Mrs. Stenberg!" Mr. DuPree said with gusto as Mrs. DuPree followed him into the kitchen.

"Mornin'," said Grandma. She looked up at Mrs. DuPree, then strained the wrinkles back that turned down her mouth. "I was so relieved when all of you made it back last night. Safe and sound," she said.

"Oh, yes, don't we know it!" said Mrs. DuPree. "Thank you so much for putting us up in warm beds last night! You've been so kind." Mrs. DuPree tried to hug Grandma, but Grandma stiffened so the hug wouldn't take hold.

"It's the least we can do." Those were Grandma's code words for compassion. I hoped Mrs. DuPree knew that somehow.

MaryAnne and Ricky showed up in the kitchen about the same time.

"Grandma, what's for breakfast?!" Ricky demanded.

"We're having eggs, Richard," Grandma said sternly. Grandma wasn't there when Ricky was born. She didn't know that Ricky had been Richard for only three seconds. That was right before Aunt Marge called him Ricky. He'd been Ricky ever since—except to Grandma.

Soon the table was set and all were gathered again for a meal. Conversation halted less than the day before, and Grandma was as cordial as she could be with strangers in her house, which made breakfast almost pleasant.

Afterwards, we found little to do. We kids had no interest in snow. That was unusual for the first big storm of the winter. Under the circumstances, we would just as well have stayed in the house for the foreseeable future. The adults didn't understand, so we got kicked out before supper.

I shoveled the porch while Ricky cleared off the swing. MaryAnne sat down with Ricky. "Shoesth, when do you think we'll go home?"

I gazed across at the State Road that looked more like an extension of Grandpa's potato field under a blanket of white. "Not today," I said.

"I hope it's soon, otherwise we could be stuck here and not make it back for school."

"Let it snow!" I said.

"Seriously, Shoesth. What would you do if you didn't go to school?"

"Fish. Hunt. Trap. Make my own snowshoes. Pile lumber with the guys. Build a canoe. Learn how to tie flies…"

"Okay, okay!" said MaryAnne. "You still need to go to school."

"Maybe," I said, then went back to shoveling.

Ricky slid off the porch swing, then pressed his eye into a crack between two snowy boards on the porch. "I see somethin' down there," he announced, wide-eyed.

"What is it, Ricky?" asked MaryAnne.

"I think it's a fork!"

"Nice," I said. "Maybe there's a treasure down there, Ricky. Why don't you see if you can find a way in? Never know what you'll uncover!" I egged Ricky on to keep him busy outside. The adults wouldn't be too happy to have him back inside this early, and then I'd be in trouble with Mama after all that effort she put into getting him dressed.

"I can't fit through a crack," declared Ricky. "But I know where we could find a treasure!" Ricky rose to his knees, staring knowingly at MaryAnne.

"Where?" MaryAnne said, always accommodating Ricky.

"The door in your bedroom."

"*My* bedroom?" asked MaryAnne.

"Yeah. Where you slept. The door with the lock on it!" emphasized Ricky. "But you can't go in there," he said as he raised his mitten high over his head, then slapped it down to the porch, "or you'll fall *right* through!"

"You really think you'll fall through?" asked MaryAnne with a big smile.

"Yeah. Mama said!" Ricky furrowed his brow. "Mama almost fell through when *she* was a little girl."

"You're so cute, Ricky," MaryAnne said tenderly.

"I mean it!" Ricky crossed his arms, turned away, then stomped one foot. With that, he went back inside and slammed the door behind him.

"Nice going," I said.

"What did I do? All I said was that he was cute."

"He's a boy, MaryAnne. Boys don't want to be cute. Besides, Ricky always wants to be *right*." MaryAnne sighed loud enough for me to hear while I shoveled snow for Oscar's entertainment.

Then MaryAnne said, "I want to see it."

That got my shovel stopped. "See what?"

"I want to see what's in your grandma's attic. It would be something fun to do. Better than sitting out here doing nothing."

I gave MaryAnne an eye of suspicion. I was the one who had gotten us into trouble at the mill. I even had to insist that she come with me to spy on Lawrence Blankenshine. Now *she* egged *me* to snoop in Grandma's spare room?

"You're trying to get me in trouble," I said.

"What? Why would I do that?"

"Revenge."

"Revenge!?" MaryAnne got up off the swing with a face for fightin'. "Shoesth Makinen! How could you say such a thing? I thought we were best friends after what happened last summer. Now you think I'm trying to get back at you?" It was MaryAnne's turn to cross her arms, turn away, and stomp her foot on the porch.

That was the first time MaryAnne said my last name. Kinda like Mama—Mama called me Arthur or Makinen only if I was in real trouble. I didn't say nothin' for a while 'cause MaryAnne looked like she needed coolin' off. She wasn't saying anything, either. I scraped in front of the door with the shovel a couple more times for good measure. Finally, I chanced a few words to check her mood.

"So, if you aren't trying to get me in trouble, what is it?"

"Never mind. Just forget it, Shoesth."

"Fine," I said.

Only a moment passed. "Curiosity," she said. "That's all—I thought it would be something fun to do."

"Okay," I said, wanting to smooth things over, since we didn't need any more conflict at Grandma's. "It's dark in there. I'll have to get the lantern from the cellar so we can see." We tiptoed inside, and I quickly retrieved the lantern from the cellar.

Inside the entry, I could hear the adults talking in the front room. Ricky's voice was mixed in there too. We took off our coats and boots, then tiptoed down the hallway.

"Wait," I whispered. I turned back to the kitchen to grab a couple matches from the box on the wall, then caught up to MaryAnne. Once in the back bedroom, I lit the lamp, blew out the match, and adjusted the wick. I quietly lifted the padlock and flipped open the latch. Rusty hinges squeaked loudly as the door opened halfway on its own. MaryAnne's eyes widened to see inside. My heart pounded—not so much about what we might find, but about being caught. I held the lamp forward before we dared make another move. Kneeling down, we both put our heads through the door's opening. Inside were floor joists without a floor. Underneath the joists was what must have been the top of the ceiling below—skinny strips of wood Dad called lathe, with plaster squishing through. The place smelled old. Older than Grandpa. Boards lay across the joists in places where boxes and wooden crates were stored. Looked like lots of dusty junk. A few canning jars were near the door— likely jars that didn't get used that fall. There were three short boards nearby big enough to stand on.

"Follow me," I said, as I stepped forward in squat positon. I made my way onto the second board, then balanced one foot on a joist, careful not to fall. Squatting down, MaryAnne followed suit. I was afraid she'd trip on her dress.

"Kinda creepy," MaryAnne said.

"Just an old attic. Looks like Grandma's stuff," I said, poking at a crate that held old pine cones on a red ribbon. MaryAnne teetered her way to a small trunk with a piece of cloth hanging from the corner of its closed lid.

"What's in here?" MaryAnne pondered as she jimmied the trunk's latch. MaryAnne lifted the lid, then gasped. "Bring the lantern here."

I watched my step to accommodate her.

"Look at this dress, Shoesth. It's beautiful!" MaryAnne said as she held up the top of a piece of clothing that looked older than time. "Isn't it lovely?" she said, looking at me for approval.

I raised an eyebrow.

"Pale blue. I could see your grandma wearing this to a fancy ball," MaryAnne said.

"I don't think you should dig in there," I warned. The girl was making me nervous.

"I'm not," she said. "I just want to see this." MaryAnne stood on her wobbly board as tall as she could, bent over at the waist on account of the rafters. She held the top of the dress to her neck as she flung the rest of the mass out of the trunk.

"What was that?" I wondered aloud as something flew out with the dress and settled between two joists.

"What?"

"Be careful," I said. "You threw something else out of the trunk. Put the dress back, MaryAnne. You're going to get us in trouble." MaryAnne began to pile the folds of cloth back into the trunk while I looked for what else came out. Lying on top of the slats below the joists was a folded paper, probably as old as the dress by the looks of it. I picked it up and opened it out of curiosity.

MaryAnne had finished her packing. "What's that?" she asked.

"It says 'My dearest Alma . . .' Looks like a letter to my grandma."

"Can I see?"

I handed the paper to MaryAnne, then held the light up while she read the letter out loud.

June 12, 1883

My Dearest Alma,

It has been too long since we've spoken. I have to tell you that Stoney Creek is a lonely place when you're not here. Please know that I love you more than words can say. You are a treasure that I pray to have one day, but until we bear the same yoke; a treasure beyond my reach. I so desire you, yet I cannot disobey God.

But there is hope, Alma—we've spoken of it before. Heaven is like a treasure to be sought after. I pray that you find the Truth so we may be equally yoked and live a joyful life together—yet not by my will. I am prepared to give you all that I have; to lay it at the foot of the cross, so that you may know my love for you.

Again, the kingdom of heaven is like unto treasure hid in a field; the which when a man hath found, he hideth, and for joy thereof goeth and selleth all that he hath, and buyeth that field.

Praying you find the Treasure.

Love,
Isaac

"Is Isaac your grandpa?" MaryAnne asked.

"No. Grandpa's name is Aleksander. Grandma calls him Alek."

"Then who is Isaac?"

"Beats me."

"Did your grandma ever find the Treasure?"

"MaryAnne, you're asking me?! It's just some love letter from way back in time. Put it back and let's get outta here."

"It could be a real treasure, Shoesth. Plus, we should find out if your grandma ever found *thee* treasure."

"What are you talking about?"

"The Treasure of heaven. Did your grandma find that out?"

"*You* go ask her," I said.

"Shoesth," MaryAnne insisted in a loud whisper, "this guy Isaac might be writing about a real hidden treasure. I think we should find out what happened."

"We can't take the letter," I snapped.

"Let me copy it, then. It'll only take a minute. There's a pencil and paper at the writing table. I'll do it real fast!"

MaryAnne was out the door before I could say, "Now hold on." I left the lantern lit inside the attic, closed the door, then stood watch at the top of the stairs while MaryAnne scribbled.

"Hurry up," I whispered. More scribbling. Finally, MaryAnne finished.

"Okay, let's put it back," she said.

We scurried across the loose boards, lifted the trunk lid, slipped the letter in, and then backed out carefully. I turned the lantern wick down until it snuffed out. Then I hung the padlock on the latch and took a deep breath.

"Hey, whatcha doin'?"

MaryAnne gasped at Ricky's voice. I jumped so hard I nearly dropped the lantern.

"Nothin', Ricky," I said. "Just looking around."

"What's the lamp for?"

"Never mind!" I turned to MaryAnne. "Let's go downstairs and see what everyone's doing." We left Ricky there to put distance between us and his imagination. MaryAnne and I joined big people still visiting in the front room.

"There they are," Mama said, changing the subject to put attention on us. "Where have you two been?"

"Just talking," I said.

"Talking? About what? What do you and MaryAnne talk about these days?" Mama prodded, then smiled slyly at Grandma.

"Oh, a whole lot of stuff and a whole lot of nothin'," I said, covering for both of us.

"Now if that doesn't sound just like a man!" Mama said as she laughed with the other ladies. I was glad to take the brunt, still feeling guilty of the exploration MaryAnne and I had gotten into.

"Toivo, dear! When do you think we'll be able to leave Ma and Pa and let them have their house back to themselves?"

CRASH!!

Dad had no time to answer. A piece of plaster the size of my foot fell onto Grandma's lap. Smaller chunks scattered across the floor while plaster dust covered Grandma's head, turning her hair whiter than it already had been. Grandma ducked. Mama screeched. Grandpa yelled, "What in tarnation is going on up there?!" Ricky's leg hung through the ceiling up to the middle of his thigh. His other knee pressed through the same hole, forcing several pieces of lathe to protrude down into the room like unwelcome daggers. Ricky's pants were torn, revealing a gash on his calf that oozed blood.

Reeling from shock, we paused for a brief moment of silence before the scream that was heard clear to Maple Hill.

4

Home at Last

Come morning, Dad was looking for creative ways to get us home. He talked about loading us all on Grandpa's powder sled again. Mama wasn't liking that, but tension in the house grew high enough to make nearly anything a possibility.

After breakfast, Dad and Grandpa fashioned a temporary patch on the ceiling while Mama fashioned another patch on Ricky's calf. Ricky was actually hurt, for a change. He was taking it well considering how even the smallest boo-boo could shake up his life.

"Are you feeling better today, Ricky?" asked MaryAnne. Ricky puckered his lips and nodded his head ever so slightly. I could tell by his screams last night that "falling through" would stick with Ricky until he grew too old to have a memory. He was in enough trouble with Dad, Mama, Grandpa, and especially Grandma, to last him that long too.

"You need to control that boy!" Grandma had said to Mama last night. Then she started talking Swedish again. I stayed away from her and she hadn't shown herself much after that.

Me and MaryAnne figured Ricky didn't know that we had been in Grandma's attic, otherwise he would have squealed on us for sure. Either way, we weren't talking about it. I wanted to forget the whole thing and go home.

It hadn't snowed much at all since I shoveled the porch the day before. I put on my things and went outside for fresh air. Fresh, peaceful air. The sun shone for the first time in three days, making it difficult to see without squinting. Off in the distance, I heard a faint rumble of an engine. As it grew louder, I realized something was coming down the State Road from Maple Hill. Then I saw the plume of white, and the top of a plow's wedge breaking a path through nearly three feet of snow. The jangle of tire chains was a welcome sound as the plow rumbled past Grandpa's driveway.

"Dad! The plow went by!" I announced after flinging the kitchen door open. Dad and Grandpa already had their boots on and were donning coats and hats.

"I heard, Shoe. Let's get the horses and hitch up the sleigh." All three horses were hitched and ready in record time.

Grandpa drove Tater, pulling the rest of us—same way we'd arrived two days before. This time we brought shovels and our own horses tied to the back of the rig. We found our wagon seat jutting out of a snowbank, with the rest of the wagon buried by the plow. Somehow the plow driver managed his way past, narrowly missing our wagon.

It only took us about an hour to dig out and hitch up. Unlike our last departure, we were all quite eager to be in the back of a lumber wagon, ready to leave. We waved to Grandpa and said good-bye to the longest Thanksgiving on record.

***

Monday was upon me like a Thanksgiving storm. Fifth grade had been trouble enough, but sixth came with more schoolwork than a guy should have to endure. Math had a new thing called "story problems." I wasn't much for stories, as you know. I liked things the way they really were. Mr. Hooper didn't see it that way. He was full of stories that always seemed to have a difficult math problem tangled up in there. If it weren't for math, then there was a history lesson to be dug from the pages of a story Mr. Hooper wanted to read. I spent many a morning reminiscing on Mrs. LeMarche and her beads.

Mr. Hooper was our first man. All us kids were seated on the first day of class when our new teacher walked in the room. "It's a man!" exclaimed Becky Rinken, loud enough for everyone to hear.

"We can all see that," I retorted.

Becky wasn't much for an argument. She smiled back at me, embarrassed. I don't know why Becky sat right behind me that first day. Maybe she figured teacher would move us around as always. But not Mr. Hooper. He left the seating arrangement up to us—Mark Badeau in front of me (the kid that I sat behind in fifth grade until MaryAnne barged in), and Becky behind. So there sat Becky with most of the boys for the rest of the year. There's a good side to everything—at least it wasn't Buffalo Alice. Buffalo had made it past fifth grade on her second try, so she moved on with the rest of us to sixth. Nobody flunked last year. We had all learned enough to be in sixth grade, and we had all gotten bigger, too—especially Buffalo Alice. Her age wasn't going to catch up to her size anytime soon, near as I could see. It was clear that she made out quite well at the Koskelas after her Ma and Pa got thrown in the clink. Buffalo had found a desk at the back of the room near the girls' side, so it was just as well that Becky sat behind me.

Monday recess seemed better than other days of the week. Probably because it was Monday. MaryAnne found me by the flagpole.

"Thought about the letter at all?"

"No." Truth was, I hadn't. I was still unnerved by it. Any bit of thinkin' on the attic got me more aggravated at MaryAnne for getting us into the whole mess.

"Ricky wouldn't have fallen through if we didn't go in Grandma's attic," I said.

"Yeah, I know."

"And you got us in there."

"Shoesth! I was the one that said never mind, then you lit the lantern and got us in!"

"And who took out the dress and nearly got us caught snooping?"

MaryAnne looked at me incredulously. "Really! It wasn't like *you* weren't there!"

Never argue with a redhead, I thought.

MaryAnne's voice softened. "We're in this together, you know."

I didn't want to be *in* anything. MaryAnne was curiously intent on the content of that letter—as if it held more than what had been written in those few words.

"You really think there's a treasure?"

"I do, Shoesth. I've read the letter over and over. Isaac was pleading for your grandma to find the Treasure of heaven. I want to know if she did." MaryAnne stared intently at me as if to peer into my soul.

"So what? When she comes to visit, you can ask her, all right?"

"I think there was more." MaryAnne pursed her red lips like she held a big secret I was supposed to plead from her. I said nothing.

"I think Isaac hid a treasure for your grandma to prove his love to her," she continued. "We have to find out who Isaac is and if your grandma ever found it."

"Wow. You've really been thinking about this."

"Ever since we got home."

"But, MaryAnne, how are we going to find out stuff without people knowing we got into Grandma's attic?" I asked. "Ricky's the only one that's been in Grandma's attic, as far as anyone else knows—and I want to keep it that way."

"Yeah." MaryAnne pondered. "The letter was written in 1883. We need to find someone from Stoney Creek back then."

"Mrs. Krebbs."

"Mrs. Krebbs?" MaryAnne asked. "I thought you didn't like Mrs. Krebbs."

"I didn't say I liked her. I said she might have been here back then. I think she's older than Grandma. Dad said Mr. and Mrs. Krebbs homesteaded here before lumbering came to town."

"Then you'll find a way for us to meet with Mrs. Krebbs?" MaryAnne gave me her upside-down smile— smiling with her eyes at the same time. Funny how she did that. The recess bell rang just as Buffalo Alice sauntered by.

"Time for class, lovebirds."

I clenched my jaw at Buffalo. MaryAnne ignored Buffalo Alice and changed her smile at me into a dimpled grin. I didn't know *what* to think about that.

5

The Last Time I Cried

"I found it, Shoesth!" cried MaryAnne. "I found the verse in Dad's Bible last night—the one that's in Isaac's letter!" MaryAnne pulled out the copy of the letter from her writing tablet. "See?" MaryAnne began to read, "'Again, the kingdom of heaven is like unto treasure hid in a field; the which when a man hath found, he hideth, and for joy thereof goeth and selleth all that he hath, and buyeth that field.' That's Matthew 13:44!"

"Okay," I said.

"It's another clue, Shoesth. There's got to be more clues. When are we going to talk with Mrs. Krebbs?" she pressed.

A meeting with Mrs. Krebbs was about as likely as being struck by lightning in the dead of winter. For one, Mrs. Krebbs wasn't in her yard talking to her flowers or hanging out her laundry in December. And two, what would it take for me to arrange a meeting with her and MaryAnne anyway?

Whenever we saw each other at church, MaryAnne gave me the look—kinda the way someone looks when they want you to do something but they can't say it. Mrs. Krebbs was there every Sunday, but I was not about to make a scene.

"Shoesth," MaryAnne scolded me after church just before Christmas, "when are we going to ask Mrs. Krebbs about Isaac?"

"I don't know. We can't just trap her in the entry and start a conversation about someone she might not even know. Do *you* want to do that?"

"You need to be there, Shoesth. It's your grandma. Besides, you said you would find a way for us to meet with Mrs. Krebbs."

"I did?"

"Shoesth, it's been a whole month, and we have nothing new," MaryAnne said impatiently.

"Yeah, I know. Even if we did, we can't dig for treasure in the winter."

MaryAnne's stern look left me perplexed. We had been best friends. Now Oscar looked pretty good again. I didn't understand MaryAnne's passion for the letter. I had hoped she was right, merely for the excitement of it all. But what about Grandpa? Does he know? How would he feel if this Isaac guy really did do something like that to show his love toward Grandma?

"I still feel guilty about taking the letter," I said.

"We didn't take it. We put it back, remember?" MaryAnne justified.

"Why are you so enthralled with it?" I asked.

"Don't you see? Shoesth, it's the most beautiful love story. Isaac wanted your grandma to know Jesus so the two of them could marry. I think he laid up a treasure for her—to prove it!"

I didn't see it. I didn't understand how a guy could be infatuated with Grandma. Maybe she was young once—or even pretty. But why would a guy be that concerned about how much Grandma loved Jesus? Couldn't they just go to church together? Couldn't they have married anyway? What *did* pique my interest was why Grandma didn't like the guy. Maybe he was some kind of creep.

"MaryAnne, we're not going talk to Mrs. Krebbs without making it obvious to my mom and dad—and your mom and dad. You'll have to be patient."

"Fine, Shoesth. I will consider this a trying of my patience."

The more I got to know MaryAnne, the more of a mystery she became to me. Maybe girls about to turn twelve were like that. Half of sixth grade was girls turning twelve—and getting more complicated every day.

Perhaps that's why Mark and I spent a lot more time together. Both of us were trappin' weasels. Since Mark's farm was on the other side of Red Town, I decided to set all my traps up his way. I had made two more weasel boxes, so I had six traps set along fences, by chicken coops, and in the old buildings nobody used anymore. Mark had five.

Sometimes we checked all our traps together, sometimes we went our own ways. But every day before school we let each other know how we were doing.

"Any luck yesterday?" Mark asked, rubbing his hand over his prickly buzz cut.

"One tripped, and bait gone out of two boxes, but no weasels."

The trapping report, as I called it, was almost as exciting as opening the lids on my weasel boxes. By late January it was clear that Mark was a better skinner than me. I had cut small holes in two of the four hides I had stretched. None of Mark's had holes in them. He had caught four weasels too, but would get better money for them on account of their hides were skinned perfectly. It was a good trappin' year. Girls just didn't understand that. So me and Mark found lots of things to do together.

He and I each managed to rustle up a pair of skates. We spent a lot of time shoveling off the mill pond then skating on the area we cleared. We did a lot of that—mostly shoveling, because it snowed so often, especially in February. We were winded by the time the rink was cleared, so we had enough in us to race around the rink a few times before hoofing it back home. One thing nice about Mark, same that I liked about Oscar, was that he didn't say much. That meant we didn't disagree much either, and that was just as well with me. I got home late one evening and dropped my skates near the door.

"They're coming faster, Toivo, and—" said Mama, holding her big belly with one hand and the edge of the kitchen chair with the other.

"And what?" Dad asked. Mama wasn't saying anything. But her eyes were saying she didn't like whatever was coming. I froze in the doorway, wondering what to do. After holding her breath for a time, Mama finally spoke again.

"And harder, Toivo. Faster and harder. Get Mrs. Johnson and go get the doc." Dad moved more quickly than the night Ricky got lost hunting grasshoppers. He had only gotten one boot on when Mama pled, "Hurry!"

Dad was out the door with his coat in hand. Mama looked at Ricky, who had come to the bottom of the stairs to see what was going on. "Ricky, get upstairs and don't come back down." Then Mama turned to me with wide eyes. "Shoe, help me to the bedroom." I was stunned that Dad had left me like this. "Now!" she yelled.

I came into the kitchen with my boots on to help Mama. She had grabbed her belly again and went stiff as a statue. *Where was Aunt Marge?* I thought. Last time a baby came, Aunt Marge showed up from nowhere to take me away. Mama's face grimaced with pain. That's when I noticed blood on the floor. Thin blood. Like water and blood. I thought Mama was going to die. Finally, Mama spoke again.

"Now, Shoe!"

I lifted hard under one of Mama's arms. She wasn't going anywhere. I got behind her, grabbed under both arms and heaved as hard as I could. Mama got up on her feet—sort of. She was on her feet and half her weight was still on me. I hobbled her through the front room to her bedroom door, then helped her onto the bed and put a blanket over her. The bed didn't seem to help. Mama got stiff again. Only this time, she grunted, wailed, and then screamed, all in succession.

I left the room. I paced to the kitchen then back to Mama's bedroom door, then back to the kitchen again. Ricky appeared at the bottom of the stairs.

"What's happenin'?"

"Get back upstairs, Ricky."

"Why is Mama crying?"

"She's having a baby! Get back upstairs right now!"

Where was Mrs. Johnson? How long would it take for Dad to come with the doctor? Mama had gone quiet again. That worried me. Then the wailing started up. Those sounds were as torture to my ears. Twice, a quiet pause, then the third time, and silence again.

"Arthur! Come in here!" Mama yelled.

I entered the bedroom in shock at what met my eyes. Mama's face dripped sweat and tears. She held a wet baby as gray as ash from the stove. The baby's belly was attached to a thick, wrinkled cord that extended from underneath the blanket. Mama struggled to sit up.

"Help me up!" Mama said with urgency in her voice.

I supported her arm as she sat up against the wall as best she could. Then Mama held the lifeless child by the feet and spanked its bottom. Nothing happened. She did it again, only harder this time. It hurt, by the sound of it. The baby choked, then cried like a little lamb—a bleating cry, followed by a gasp of air; again and again. In moments the baby's skin turned purple, then pink as my palm.

"Shoe, this is your baby sister," Mama announced.

I could see that. She came out with no clothes on. I didn't say anything to Mama. I couldn't. The last time I cried was when I opened the box that held my puppy, Oscar. All I could do now was choke back tears. I wasn't sure why, but I cried like the new baby in Mama's arms. Mama pulled me close.

"I love you, Arthur."

I hadn't heard that in a long time. I soaked in Mama's hug until she said, "Shoe, go into the entry, quickly. There's spare fishing line on the shelf in the closet. Bring it here with the scissors. We've got to tie off this cord."

I found fishing line and the scissors just as Mrs. Johnson came through the door without knocking.

"Where's your ma?"

"In the bedroom," I said.

"And how's she coming along," Mrs. Johnson said as she unbuttoned her coat.

"She had the baby already."

"What?! Lord have mercy!" Mrs. Johnson scurried past me with her coat and boots still on. I followed.

"Oh, my goodne-e-ess!" exclaimed Mrs. Johnson. "We have to get that cord tied." I handed her the spool of line and scissors, then went back to find Ricky. In the kitchen, I paused at the calendar on the wall. February 27, 1925. *A day I will never forget*, I thought.

Ricky stood at the bottom of the stairs again. "You have a new sister, Ricky."

"Re-e-eally?! What's her name?"

"I don't think she has a name yet."

"No name?! A kid with no name?!"

"Let's go see," I said, leading Ricky to the bedroom. The baby was bundled in a blanket when we got there.

"Want to see your new baby sister, Ricky?" Mama asked. Ricky edged to the side of the bed and peered inside the bundle of blankets. Then he fell back, wide-eyed.

"What's her name?" said Ricky.

"Her name is Sophie. Sophie Olivia Makinen."

"Wow! That's a big name for a little kid," said Ricky.

I thought the name fit just right.

6

Trapped

"I got one!" My heart raced with excitement as Mark and I stumbled across the dam. Deep beneath the clear, cold water was the dead body of a beaver caught in a trap. "Let's pull it up," I said.

We both jerked on the tag alder pole until it slid loose from the muck at the bottom of the pond. My hands shook as I squeezed ice-cold steel springs to release the beaver's paw. With aching fingers, I straightened the drowning wire, drove the pole back in the pond, and then carefully re-set the pan's trigger while keeping my cold fingers out of the jaws.

"Wow. Nice beaver," observed Mark as I held it up by its tail. The weight of the animal gave me a sense of satisfaction. "Where are you going to stretch it?"

"On the wall in the woodshed. I've got the perfect spot for it." I already had pictured where my first beaver pelt would be tacked up to dry. "Don't you wish you had a trap too, Mark?"

Mark rubbed his prickly hair again. "Yeah, but I'm saving up for a steer to raise and butcher come fall."

Weasel season had passed. Mark and I had pulled our traps three weeks earlier before the fur buyer came to town. Word must have gotten out because trappers came out of nowhere—enough to form a line, waiting to sell their furs.

We waited our turn, gazing at the hides in the back of the truck. Beaver pelts were piled as high as my waist. Coyote and raccoon skins hung from both walls. Even an otter had met its fate with the other dead animals.

I didn't recognize the stocky man in front of me—or the smell. My nose twitched from a repugnant odor that was stronger than the smell of dried animal skins. The trapper wore a dirty, red hat and a stained brown coat. He held a rope over his back that threaded through eye-holes of ten or more beaver pelts. He grabbed the load and dropped it onto the buyer's table.

"Top price. That's what I come fer," the man growled. He turned to the side, revealing a bulging, hair-covered bottom lip. He spit a long stream of brown juice onto the dirt, then pushed his lower lip out even further.

The buyer never looked up. Instead, he inspected each hide carefully, pulling one from the bottom of the stack. "A lot of scars," he said, pointing to thin areas on the hide from past injuries.

"They're worth top price, I tell ya," said the trapper.

"Where else you gonna go with these?" asked the fur buyer. "Processors are looking for clear pelts, no fat, scar-free. I'll give you a dollar for these two and four apiece fer the others." The buyer added numbers in a ledger while the trapper huffed and turned toward me and Mark. Brown saliva dribbled from the corner of his mouth. He clenched his jaw until the red hairs of his beard stood on end. "That'll make thirty-four dollars total," concluded the buyer. The trapper spun back around.

"Thirty four!" he yelled. "These'll fetch sixty—at least! You dirty, rotten thief, I'm gonna…" the angry man reached out to grab the fur buyer's coat, knocking the table over in between them. A lanky guy jumped out of the truck as two other men grabbed hold of the trapper. I stepped back as Mark turned to leave.

"Get back here, Mark," I urged. Mark stopped, then turned around to watch from the edge of the lantern's light.

One of the men holding the trapper's arm said, "Take your hides and get outta here, Snuffy." The trapper considered his adversaries, then pulled away. He picked up his beaver pelts.

"You're not gonna hear the end of this, you dirty, rotten scoundrels! Thirty-four dollars—enough to drive a man…" His voice trailed off into the darkness.

The fur buyer stood his table upright and was back in business with the next man in line.

Thirty-four dollars, I thought. *What I could do with thirty-four dollars.* It was then that I decided where my weasel earnings would go. I took a trip to the Co-op the very next morning.

"Hi, Mr. Saddlekamp."

"Well hello, Shoe. Good Saturday morning to ya."

"Do you still have beaver traps?" I asked.

"Sure do! Genuine Victor—only two left."

"I'll take one, sir." That was all I could afford if I wanted some pocket money left over.

"Planning on doing some beaver trapping, are ya?" asked Mr. Saddlekamp as I paid for my prize.

"Yup. Me and Mark Badeau. Except he doesn't have any traps yet."

"Well, send him over. You tell Mark I've got one left— just for him."

"I will, sir." I turned to leave, then remembered the night before. "Mr. Saddlekamp?"

"Yes, Shoe."

"What do you know about a guy named Snuffy?"

"Snuffy?"

"Yeah. He smelled real bad. And he tried starting a fight with the fur buyer last night 'cause he didn't like his price. The guys called him Snuffy."

"Oh, you must be talking about Clem." Mr. Saddlekamp's face lit up. "Clem Ruskin. He comes in here every couple weeks. Always picks up snuff to chew—I can count on that."

"So that's why they call him Snuffy?"

"I suppose, that would make sense." Mr. Saddlekamp looked deep in thought. "Don't go setting that new trap of yours around him. I'd stay clear if I were you."

"Where's he trap?"

"Clem's a hermit. Folks say he lives south of Red Town—a squatter on Forestry land is what he is. Clem's probably got a line set on the South Branch. Just stick around here with your trappin'—you'll be fine."

"Got it!" I thanked Mr. Saddlekamp for the advice, turned for the door, but then paused with another thought in mind.

"Is there something else, Shoe?"

"Have you ever heard of Isaac from Stoney Creek?" I asked.

"Isaac?" Mr. Saddlekamp shook his head. "Can't say that I have."

"Never mind, it's not important." I rushed out the door and ran my new trap all the way home.

***

School was nearly over when I came across Mrs. Krebbs in her garden. She was digging up dead plants that she had talked to last season. I saw a perfect opportunity, so I stopped walkin' before she saw me. MaryAnne hadn't given up hope that I would arrange a meeting with Mrs. Krebbs. She had asked me once a week all winter, it seemed. Our chance was right before me. All I needed to do was to catch MaryAnne on her way home.

I returned to the main road where I spied red hair in the distance, glimmering in the sun. But were my eyes playing tricks? MaryAnne was dwarfed by Buffalo Alice at her side. What was she doing with her?

As the two of them approached, I said, "MaryAnne, we have to talk."

Buffalo responded first, "The two of you have to talk, do you? O-o-o-o!" Buffalo raised her eyebrows at MaryAnne, then gave me a big, toothy grin. I blenched. It was the first time I saw Buffalo Alice smile in … ever, I think.

"What was that all about?" I asked MaryAnne as Buffalo lumbered toward her home at the Koskelas.

"What?"

"Why were you walking with her?"

MaryAnne must have thought that my question didn't deserve an answer, or perhaps she didn't understand.

"Nobody likes Buffalo," I said. "Is she your new friend or something?"

"There's nothing wrong with talking to Alice."

"Depends on what you're talking about. You'd better not be giving her any ideas," I warned.

"Ideas? What kind of ideas?! Alice doesn't know what it's like to have a friend because she's never had one. Especially a friend that's a boy. So Alice assumes that, well, you know—that we like each other." MaryAnne smiled so softly it tore down all my defenses.

I stuck to my blank stare.

MaryAnne's smile faded. "We're still friends, aren't we?"

"Of course we're still friends."

"So is *that* what you wanted to talk to me about?" MaryAnne asked.

The sight of Buffalo in the road made me forget why I had come out to meet MaryAnne.

"No!" I said. "I saw Mrs. Krebbs working in her garden. I think we've got her trapped."

7

A Most Beautiful Love Story

"Oh, hello, Arthur—and Miss DuPree—what a fine day it is to see you," said Mrs. Krebbs. I knew we didn't have to be the first to offer a greeting. All we needed was to bait her with our presence, then Mrs. Krebbs would bite. She did. So instead of walking faster past Mrs. Krebbs' house, MaryAnne and I stepped into her yard.

Mrs. Krebbs stopped shoveling. "What can I do for the two of you?"

"We were wondering if you could tell us about somebody," I said.

"Well, that depends." Mrs. Krebbs squinted at me through her wrinkles. "I don't like gossip. That's not the Christian thing to do."

"It's not gossip," said MaryAnne. "We're trying to find out some history about Stoney Creek."

"History—now that's something I know a little about—being the old girl that I am." Mrs. Krebbs smiled wryly. "What sort of history?"

MaryAnne was ready to burst, and I was more than willing to let her talk. "We want to know about Isaac," blurted MaryAnne.

"Isaac? You mean Abraham's Isaac? He was a Godly man—father of Jacob, you know. Did you come here today to talk about Jesus?"

MaryAnne worried a look at me while I wondered what passage we were on. "Um, no ma'am," MaryAnne replied. "I mean, we would love to talk about Jesus, and Isaac of the Bible, but we were thinking about another Isaac—Isaac of Stoney Creek."

I was uncomfortable with how freely MaryAnne was throwing the word *we* around. What did she mean that I would love to talk about Jesus and the Bible?

"Isaac of Stoney Creek," pondered Mrs. Krebbs, leaning heavier on her shovel. "There's no Isaac in these parts."

MaryAnne glanced my way again. I took the opportunity to signal an exit, motioning with my head. "Maybe he moved," MaryAnne continued. Her ignoring me said that MaryAnne wasn't going to let go of Mrs. Krebbs as long as she held hope for a clue.

"We should be going," I interjected, having no more appetite for MaryAnne's prodding.

MaryAnne continued to disregard my presence. "Could have been a long time ago," she said.

The scowl on Mrs. Krebb's brow cleared, shallowing her permanent wrinkles. "You're not talking about Isaac..." Mrs. Krebbs looked around the yard as she talked to herself. "What was his surname? Borg," she said. "You're not talking about Isaac Borg, are you?"

"I don't know," MaryAnne said sheepishly. Her mouth hung agape, holding out for another word from the old woman.

Mrs. Krebbs' scowl returned. "Mr. Borg lived here a long time ago—ever so briefly. Are you sure it's him you want to know about?"

"Maybe," MaryAnne said. "If he lived in Stoney Creek, then that's probably him!"

Mrs. Krebbs put her shovel back to work turning dirt on top of leaves and dead flowers crushed by last winter's snow. Soon her back was to us as she moved down a neat row of fresh dirt. I figured our meeting time was over.

"Ps-s-st." I finally got MaryAnne's attention, rolled my eyes back toward the road, and then mouthed, "Let's go."

MaryAnne glared. Just as I was about to leave by myself, Mrs. Krebbs stopped digging and turned around. "Why do you want to know?" she asked.

MaryAnne set her books on the ground, opened her writing tablet, and pulled out the paper she had written in Grandma's attic. She must have taken it everywhere, by the looks of it. MaryAnne straightened the crease at its middle, then brought it to Mrs. Krebbs.

The elderly woman stood her shovel in the dirt, took the paper, and then held it out as far as her arm would reach. She read aloud, almost to herself.

June 12, 1883

My Dearest Alma,

It has been too long since we've
spoken. I have to tell you that
Stoney Creek is a lonely place
when you're not here. Please know
that I love you…

Mrs. Krebbs' voice trailed off as she turned her back and read silently to herself. An afternoon breeze tossed what was left of her wispy white hair.

I agonized in wait.

Suddenly, she gasped. Shuddering, she dropped the letter onto the freshly tilled dirt, then put her hand to her mouth. MaryAnne touched her shoulder and tried to peer into her face.

"Is everything okay?"

Mrs. Krebbs' hand wiped one eye. "I need to sit down, my dear," she tremored. "Help me into the house." MaryAnne held the old woman's arm as the two of them shuffled to the front door. MaryAnne furrowed at me to pick up her letter from the dirt and follow her in.

I wanted to run. There was nothing inside Mrs. Krebbs' house that interested me. Nor was I interested in learning how we made an old woman cry. I considered the road again.

"Shoesth!" MaryAnne's eyes implored me to follow. Not wanting to play the coward, I grabbed the paper from the garden, then ran to the porch and held the door.

Inside, Mrs. Krebbs settled in one of the two chairs at a small kitchen table that held two placemats and an old candle for a centerpiece. The room was tidier than MaryAnne's house and it looked to have only the bare necessities a cook might need. I leaned against the sink, wondering how long we were trapped in such a place. MaryAnne sat in the other chair, looking to comfort Mrs. Krebbs. The woman's wrinkles wept tears. She pulled a hanky from the sleeve of her dress to dab her eyes.

"That was Isaac Borg."

MaryAnne glanced at me. She'd been wide-eyed since Mrs. Krebbs first uttered the name Borg.

"What happened to him, Mrs. Krebbs?"

She dabbed her eyes again, then turned to me. "Does your grandmother know about this, Arthur?"

I shook my head. "No, ma'am."

"How *is* your grandmother?"

"Fine. I think she's better when me and Ricky aren't there," I said. The image of Grandma with plaster-colored hair haunted me.

"You boys are trying her, are you?"

I didn't say anything. Mrs. Krebbs didn't need to know about Ricky falling through, about the blood—or the scream. The woman purposed to regain her composure.

"Oh, I shouldn't trouble you children with such things. Besides, that water passed over the dam decades ago."

"But we want to know, Mrs. Krebbs. It's quite all right," pressed MaryAnne.

"Silly of me to be weeping so many years later," she continued. "I suppose it's because nobody wanted to talk about it—not even your mother, Arthur." The woman blew her nose louder than I expected a lady should. "I haven't spoken with Alma since she married your granddaddy." Mrs. Krebbs looked at me like *I* did something wrong. "That letter answered a lot of questions—and resurfaced a bushel of old feelings. Can I see it again?" I placed the paper on the table. Mrs. Krebbs read silently. At the end of it she whispered, "Praying you find the Treasure." Then leaning toward MaryAnne, she asked, "Where did you get the letter, MaryAnne?"

MaryAnne waited a few long seconds. "It fell out of a storage chest and then I copied it because..." MaryAnne stopped as the old woman looked at her sternly. Then she blurted, "...because it was the most beautiful love story!"

The old woman leaned back. "That, it was." She swallowed hard as her wrinkles moistened again. "A beautiful, *tragic* love story."

MaryAnne sat as still as Oscar pointing on a bird. Then she opened her mouth. "I'm so sorry. We didn't mean to make you cry."

"It's not yours to be sorry about."

Then, being careful not to press too hard, MaryAnne asked in her gentlest voice, "Where's Isaac now?" The old woman crumpled her handkerchief and wiped her face again. Then with a blank look in her eye, she lamented, "He's dead."

8

Isaac Borg

Those words, *He's dead*, flashed me back to the night Mrs. Johnson pushed open our door to report a discovery of the Stueck brothers in the hot pond. Then MaryAnne came to town and everything changed. I wanted to leave well enough alone with Mrs. Krebbs, but it seemed we had uncovered something bigger than both of us. And MaryAnne wasn't about to let go.

"What happened?" she asked.

"It's a long story, my child. Are you sure you want to hear it?"

"Oh, but we do!" MaryAnne tucked her hair behind both ears, readying to take in every word. Then she glanced at me. "Don't we, Shoesth?"

By the looks of it, I wasn't going to have a choice.

"Well, it started less than a year after Abe and I—that was my late husband, you know—after Abe and I began our homestead here at Stoney Creek. Let's see now, that would have been the year 1884. We were young then." Mrs. Krebbs emphasized by shaking her head. "My, oh my. Abe was 31 and I was just 29—still his young bride, you know, though we'd been married nigh 10 years." She looked up with a gentle smile at MaryAnne. "There weren't many folk around in those days before lumbering came to town. Abe and I worked hard together, building that farm with our own hands. These are tough parts for farming with deep snow and long, cold winters, so when things got hard we relied on each other. Neighbors meant a whole lot more back then." Mrs. Krebbs rolled the edge of her placemat with her wrinkled fingers, then continued to talk, not looking up.

"Isaac came to Stoney Creek in the spring of '81. A hardworking young man who had done well for himself before leaving Illinois to a quieter place he could call home. Folks said he had much laid up in store, but Abe and I never saw proof of that. He kept things simple—staked a plot, south of Red Town—before Red Town was even there. You might know it—straight past the right turn in the road, just beyond into the woods."

The old woman looked at me. I shook my head and kept my mouth shut. Something told me I was hearing a piece of history that had gone largely unspoken.

"It wasn't so much woods back then," she continued. "Isaac worked hard clearing the land. He'd made himself a man-sized field for farming and for raising a family someday. Only, to Abe and me, it looked like he wouldn't get there."

Mrs. Krebbs had rolled and un-rolled the edge of her placemat several times. She stopped talking to smooth it flat.

MaryAnne interjected, "Do you mean he wasn't going to have a family?'

Mrs. Krebbs hesitated before sharing any more. She was deep in thought long enough that I began to wonder if we might not hear the rest of the story.

"I don't like to talk poorly about others. The only reason I tell you at all, is so you'll know what the Lord did with Isaac Borg." She paused again, gazed out the tiny kitchen window, then back down at her placemat. "Isaac would come to town after a long day's work, then he spent his evenings in the bar. There were many a night he got kicked out at closing. When Isaac wasn't working, he was drunk or fighting."

I tried to catch MaryAnne's eye to give her an I-told-you-so face. This Isaac guy did sound like a creep, all right. MaryAnne wasn't paying attention to me. She glued on Mrs. Krebbs like a hound on a coon tree.

"Then one Sunday morning, Abe found Isaac sleeping on our front porch," Mrs. Krebbs continued. "By the look of the shiner he had, Isaac couldn't find his way home from another Saturday brawl. We took him in, Abe gave him black coffee, and then made him sit with us through morning meeting. We were churchin' at home then on account of there weren't many churching people at Stoney Creek. Isaac probably didn't hear a word that first meeting. Abe told him he would find him again next Sunday and bring him to our house for another drying out. Isaac attended church like that for nigh six months—right there in our kitchen. Attending church didn't seem to do anything for him, though, until one cold October morning, Isaac came to our door with his Bible in hand.

"'Helen,' he told me, 'I come to talk with Abe.'

"'Abe is putting the cows out to graze,' I told him. 'Is there something I can help you with?'

"'I don't know.'

"'What's the matter, Isaac?' I asked him.

"He didn't say anything to me for a long moment, then he said, 'I want to get right with Jesus. I want to know what Nicodemus wanted to know—how do I get born again?'

"Even as I tell you now, it gives me the chills. I remember that morning like it was yesterday. Fixing to find Abe, I stopped kneading, covered the dough, then before I left the house, I asked Isaac if he understood Jesus' response to that question. He said he hadn't. So, I turned his Bible to John and left him reading what Jesus had to say to Nicodemus while I went out to summon my husband."

MaryAnne's unblinking eyes trained on Mrs. Krebbs.

"As you can imagine, Abe was just as surprised as I was," the old woman continued. "We penned our cows in the back pasture and headed toward the house. I declare, I could hear all the angels in heaven rejoicing when we entered the door. Isaac lay face down on the kitchen floor, weeping like a baby!"

MaryAnne blinked at last. Her eyes were drying mine out, just looking at her.

"Abe asked, 'Are you okay Isaac?' " said Mrs. Krebbs. "Isaac didn't answer. He couldn't. I sat at the table and hummed 'Amazing Grace' while Isaac spoke to God. I couldn't hear everything, but I knew he was talking to Jesus—right there in our kitchen! I must have hummed 'Amazing Grace' four times before Isaac got up to the table with Abe and me. A brightness overtook his eyes that I hadn't seen in a man's face before. Abe and I simply understood we were looking at a new Isaac. Abe didn't fetch Isaac for Sunday meeting after that. Isaac came on his own—never missed one. He became like family to us, much like a younger brother would be—do you know what I mean?"

My thoughts went to Ricky. I didn't see the parallel.

"Then what happened?" MaryAnne pursued.

"Well, Isaac went about asking for a lot of forgiveness. First to me and Abe, then to the folks around Stoney Creek—the ones he picked fights with or offended in any way. Abe was thinking it would wear him right down, patching up all *his* wrongs, but it appeared to give Isaac more fervor for the Lord. We rejoiced to see the new creature that Isaac had become. He had more to share about God's word in our meetings than Abe and I put together! I'd never seen anyone so intent for doin' and not just hearin'. Do you know what I mean?"

Mrs. Krebbs asked that question a lot. Most of the time I didn't know what she meant, and this was no exception. MaryAnne sat there nodding her head. I wondered if she

was just encouraging the old woman or if she really knew
what Mrs. Krebbs meant, so I called her on it.

"Really, MaryAnne? You know what that meant?"

MaryAnne started from her stupor. "Yeah," she said
with agitation in her voice. "It means being a doer of the
Word."

I was sorry I asked. MaryAnne seemed to know the
Bible like she knew her arithmetic, and that made me look
bad.

"I'm feeling a lot better now," said Mrs. Krebbs. "You
two have been so kind to listen to this old girl go on with
stories from the past. I'm sure you're needing to get on
home from school."

"Yeah," I said. MaryAnne's effort to keep the letter
alive had sprouted an interest in finding answers to
Grandma's old beau, but so far I had only heard about a guy
that had gotten churchy like Mrs. Krebbs. I was ready to be
home to be with Oscar and Ricky and Mama—and Sophie,
if she wasn't crying.

"We have time for a little more," countered MaryAnne.
I glared at her. She shot back a look that trumped my glare.

"Please?" MaryAnne pleaded with Mrs. Krebbs.

"Oh, all right," said the old woman. "If I must. Now
where was I?"

MaryAnne reminded her, "You were saying how Isaac
spent a lot of time reading his Bible."

"Oh, yes. Isaac and his Bible. He didn't just spend time
reading, he wanted to know how to use what he read. Isaac
stopped by unexpectedly several times to ask questions

about alcohol, friends, use of the tongue. It was such a delight to watch him grow in his new walk, and we could see his hankerin' to build a homestead that would be right fine for a family. He made himself a small house, a barn big enough for his plow horse and cow, and a field big enough to feed him and the animals, with food left over. And then it happened."

The old woman stopped. Staring at her placemat, coiled so tightly it should never lay flat again, she slowly, ever so slightly, shook her head from side to side. Me and MaryAnne waited for the next word. Mrs. Krebbs didn't say anything.

Finally, MaryAnne whispered, "*What* happened, Mrs. Krebbs?"

9

The Suitor

"The Svenssons moved to town," said Mrs. Krebbs.

MaryAnne looked at me like I did something wrong. I was a Finlander, but even MaryAnne knew that the Svensson name made me half-Swede. It wasn't my fault, so I shrugged my shoulders at her.

"Was that a problem?" asked MaryAnne.

The old woman squinted across the table. "No, not a problem—not at first. The Svenssons were a fine family— still are. When they came to town, Mr. Svensson took to setting up a small grinding mill on the South Branch, which Isaac found an interest in. Abe and I really knew that he found interest in the Svensson's oldest child, Alma. O-o-hoo!—Alma was a looker back then." The old woman smirked, deeply defining her crow's feet. MaryAnne's dimples popped holes in her cheeks as she turned toward me. I gaped, trying to imagine Grandma being a "looker."

Mrs. Krebbs continued, "I remember Alma's rich, brown hair. Curly, it was—made her quite distinguished with those bright-blue eyes. Her daddy kept Alma close to home since she turned heads everywhere they went. You couldn't blame the guys, really. Her daddy was very protective. I suppose that's why Alma was nearly on the shelf when the Svenssons settled. I'm guessing she had to be eighteen. Isaac knew a fine catch when he saw one, so he set himself to getting to know everything he could about Alma."

MaryAnne sat ram-rod straight on the edge of her chair, holding the end of her braid with one hand and twirling it with the other.

"And?" she asked.

"Well, Isaac found out that Alma was a sweetheart of a girl, no doubt about that—a sturdy one, too. It wasn't but a few visits before Isaac was enthralled with her, ya know. He spent a lot of time helping out at the Svensson's mill. Her daddy must not have minded it much because he gave Isaac plenty of space to visit Alma. Abe and I figured he was fixin' to marry. We were so-o-o excited!" Mrs. Krebbs grinned broadly as she gazed out the window. "Then he stopped by one evening, enormously troubled."

"'I want her… Isaac told us.

"Abe asked him, 'Then what's holdin' you back, Isaac?'

"I thought the poor man was about to cry.

"'We'd be unequally yoked,' he said.

"I was shocked. 'Are you sure?' I asked him.

"Isaac explained, 'Today we got to talking about my past. I wanted her to know that if townsfolk were telling bad stories about me, they were probably true. But I wanted Alma to know that I'm different now—figuring she'd understand what Jesus had done by givin' me a new heart. She was listenin', so I told her what happened right here in your kitchen, how I became a new man, and how I went about asking forgiveness and all. She just got real quiet on me. That's when I asked her when *she* got a new heart, and Alma took offense to that.'

"'She said, 'A new heart?! What are you talking about, Isaac? I ain't needed a new heart 'cause I never had a bad one in the first place!'

"'Then she stormed into the house. I guess I figured that anyone as sweet, as beautiful, as… as wonderful as Alma must already got a new heart.'

"'Abe and I were stunned—first that Alma didn't know the Truth, and second, 'cause we didn't know what to say to Isaac.

"'Isaac went on to tell us that he still wanted her. 'Fact is, I love her,' he said, 'more than words can say!' That poor young man was struck with lovesickness more powerful than I'd seen before—or since. He had high hopes that your grandmother would find salvation one day. I shall never forget Isaac's impassioned declaration of her, 'Maybe we can't be equally yoked now, but I'm not givin' up on my Alma.'"

By that time, MaryAnne had twirled the green ribbon right out of her braid and was making repairs. As she tied the ribbon back in, she encouraged Mrs. Krebbs.

"Go on. I must hear the rest."

"My dear child, surely it's upon the dinner hour. You two need to scurry home. Besides, I must finish my chores and tidy things up for morning tea." The old woman pushed herself up from the chair, then sat down hard again.

MaryAnne reached across the table. "Morning tea? Can I help you with something?

"Oh, no. I don't fuss much for Mrs. Johnson. She's seen this house lived-in. You never mind, and run along."

"Okay," said MaryAnne disappointedly. Then she put on puppy eyes for Mrs. Krebbs. "But when can we hear the rest of the story?"

Mrs. Krebbs conceded with a kind smile for MaryAnne, "How about we meet back here tomorrow after school—same time?"

"Oh, certainly!" chimed MaryAnne as she glanced my way. "We'll be here!" MaryAnne gathered her things as I headed out the door.

***

I entered our house moments before the mill whistle blew. The pungent smell of leeks overtook my senses so that I could nearly taste them as I entered the kitchen. Mama banged a spoon on the edge of the soup kettle.

"Leek soup for supper? My favorite," I said as I dropped my books by the wringer.

"How could you tell?" Mama teased. Sophie was tied on her hip with a dish towel, not crying for a change. "Where'd you go after school?"

"Oh, just around. I was talking with MaryAnne." I didn't want Mama to know we were anywhere close to Mrs. Krebbs' house, so I changed the subject. "Where's Ricky?"

"In his room doing time 'til he's called down to eat."

"Oh," I said. That was a bad choice for a diversion.

"So, how are you and MaryAnne getting along?" Mama pried.

"What do you mean?"

"Well, after our trip to Grandma and Grandpa's it seems you two have been at odds, just not the friends you used to be. Is everything okay?" Mama showed a bit too much interest in MaryAnne for my comfort.

"Everything's fine, Ma. I hang out with Mark now. MaryAnne's... a girl—and there's not much to do with girls."

Mama looked at me inquisitively as she shifted Sophie higher on her hip. "You said you're still talking," Mama baited.

"Talking, yes. That's mostly what MaryAnne likes to do—and that's about it."

Mama pursed and turned back to her soup. Without looking up, she said, "She's a sweet girl, Shoe."

***

I turned off the alley onto the main road to school the next morning, not far behind MaryAnne. She spied me and stopped walking so I could catch up.

"How'd you sleep?" she asked.

"Fine. Why?"

"I couldn't fall asleep last night. Mrs. Krebbs' story kept running over and over in my head. I was thinking about Isaac and his love for your grandma. We're getting closer to the treasure, Shoesth!"

"You really think there's a treasure, don't you?"

"Oh, I'm sure of it. It's the most beautiful love story—you'll see!"

I hoped MaryAnne was right. A real-life treasure hunt would be a dream come true. Yet I wasn't seeing it like MaryAnne.

"Isaac sounded like a creep," I said. "I was thinking that's why Grandma didn't marry him, but Mrs. Krebbs was convinced that he'd changed. What I don't get is the stuff about not being yoked the same. If he was so crazy about Grandma, why didn't he just marry her?"

"It's about being together in the Lord, Shoesth."

"You're talking about going to church."

"No, not really. It's about knowing the Lord, not just going to church." I could see out of the corner of my eye that MaryAnne looked straight at me.

"That's kinda weird," I said.

"It's not weird when you've got a new heart."

"All this new heart business—that's *always* going to be weird." MaryAnne fell silent. We walked farther apart—she wasn't at my shoulder as usual. Not liking MaryAnne's silence, I changed the subject. "I hope Mrs. Krebbs tells us about the treasure after school today—that's if there is a treasure," I said.

"Me too," said MaryAnne, eyes to the ground. "Don't try to rush us out of there this time, Shoesth."

"I won't—as long as she's got something good."

***

School couldn't let out early enough. MaryAnne and I walked faster than usual on our way home. She had to skip a couple times to keep up.

"I've been waiting for this all day," said MaryAnne. We turned the corner onto Mrs. Krebbs' street, then stopped in our tracks where I halted the day before. There was a covered truck parked in front of Mrs. Krebbs' house. Several people were standing outside listening to Mrs. Johnson, who spoke through her fingers over her mouth.

"It doesn't look like a good day for our visit," I thought out loud. We edged forward.

"I wonder what's the matt..." MaryAnne didn't finish her sentence because in that moment a man backed through the front door of the old woman's house, his arms straining to hold the foot end of a stretcher. When the second man struggled through, we could see that whoever was on the stretcher had been completely covered with a sheet, from head to toe.

MaryAnne gasped. We froze as the stretcher was placed in the truck and the doors slammed shut.

10

Isaac's Field

I had never been to a funeral. Black hats, dresses, and overcoats filled the church beyond the entryway. Mama made me wear my darkest pants and a borrowed black overcoat that didn't fit.

"It's fitting for the occasion," she said.

Mrs. Krebbs didn't look herself in a casket. But then, what was a dead person to look like? My mind couldn't grasp that we were talking with her the other day, and now she lay in a box, lifeless. By the time we sat down, our pew had been taken by people I didn't recognize. We ended up behind the DuPrees. An uneasiness settled on me, sitting in a different pew with countless grim faces and darkness everywhere. That's why MaryAnne's bright-red hair was too cheery an exhibit for a funeral. So was the vivid blue ribbon she had woven into the top of her braid. In similar fashion, Mrs. DuPree's black hat was offset with a light-green scarf worn around her neck. Looked like disrespect to me.

I didn't know that Mrs. Krebbs could gather such a crowd. *Perhaps she was kind to all of these*, I thought. Two men closed the casket as the pastor began to read. I didn't hear much. All I could think about was our time with Mrs. Krebbs, our planned meeting the following day, and the sudden end of it. I was interrupted from my thoughts by a congregational hymn. Then the funeral ended as abruptly as our non-visit with Mrs. Krebbs.

I stood with MaryAnne on spring's new grass under overcast skies. Pallbearers loaded the casket into a hearse then drove it to the cemetery. I looked on as others brought tables outdoors to feed the crowd.

"Whatcha thinkin'?" asked MaryAnne.

"Those were the same tables I dragged out the door with Mrs. Krebbs—just last Fourth of July." MaryAnne's arm brushed my shoulder. Her colored ribbon popped to mind. "Why didn't you wear black?" I asked.

"I am." MaryAnne looked down at her obviously new dress. "What do you mean?"

"It's a blue ribbon," I said, watching the lunch setup activities. "I should go help with chairs."

"Wait, Shoesth. You asked me why my ribbon is blue and I want to tell you."

I turned to give her my ear.

"I like to think that somewhere in heaven there is blue, more vivid than the ribbon I'm wearing. Just like my mom—green reminds her of life!"

"Mrs. Krebbs is dead."

"Oh, but Shoesth, she knew the Lord," MaryAnne said. "I cried—only because the little I got to know her, I already miss Mrs. Krebbs. But she is in heaven now—a most wonderful place. My ribbon is for joy!"

I wondered if I would ever understand MaryAnne. After a year and a half, she was as much an oddity as a friend, and her family was still very different than any I knew. Perhaps that explained her behavior, but the way she talked to me—it was a foreign language at times. I had given up on deciphering her code a while back, and had turned to help with chairs, when Mrs. Johnson's voice came into range from behind.

"Helen said she was tired, so I poured tea for the both of us. She was reminiscing about Isaac Borg, which was very strange." I glanced back. Mrs. Johnson spoke to a woman I didn't recognize.

"Who's Isaac Borg?" the woman asked.

Me and MaryAnne raised all four of our eyebrows and stood still as statues, straining for every word.

"He was a young homesteader—way back. Helen and Abe had taken him under their wing, you know. Years ago, Helen told me how he had fallen in love…" Mrs. Johnson whispered more words, then she continued, "but she didn't want him. Helen insisted he died of lovesickness. Stopped working, stopped visiting folks—even stopped eating."

"Very odd," replied the woman.

"Yes, I know. Helen said, for years there was rumor that he buried what little money he had, but you know how townsfolk are—a bit of surmising, and pretty soon everyone's got a grandiose story. A bunch of hogwash, as far as I'm concerned."

"I've known the elderly to go back in time shortly before they pass. Very odd," the woman said again.

"Precisely," said Mrs. Johnson. "As I was saying, we were having our tea while Helen spoke, almost to herself, 'Poor boy. I still hurt for that young man.' Her face looked ashen just then. I should have taken notice. But instead, I asked her, 'Why does he concern you now?' When I finished my sentence, she slumped over in her chair, then fell hard onto the kitchen floor. Oh, mercy!" Mrs. Johnson sobbed.

***

"This looks like that bend in the road!" I said without thinking.

"What bend are you talking about?" Mark asked.

"Oh, nothing. Someone mentioned about a bend in the road back here, and this must be the place. It's not important, really."

Mark looked at me in dismay, then trained his eye on the trees at the edge of the road. He carried his dad's .22— our only weapon against squirrels in our path. I wished I had a rifle. Mark's permission to carry his dad's gun was exciting enough for the both of us to have spent the last hour hunting south of Mark's house, bringing us upon Isaac's field. As we left the road to explore, we came upon a broken-down shack that had to have been Isaac's. The shack was no bigger than a chicken coop. Nearly 40 years had taken its toll on the homesteader's cabin. Mark stepped on a broken door and through the opening ahead of me. July heat intensified in the small room. A beam of sunlight cast through a single window opening, glinting off a tin cup lying on the dirt floor. I gave it a kick.

"Look at this," said Mark. In the corner of the one-room house lay a shovel with no handle. The front edge of the spade had rusted through. "Looks pretty old."

"Let me see that." I took the rusty implement from Mark, pondering if it was the spade Isaac used to bury a treasure. "I'm keeping it," I said.

"What? That old piece of junk?"

"Yeah. I might find a use for it. You can have the cup," I said, glancing over at the tin still lying in the dirt.

Mark furrowed at me. "Right!"

"Let's check out the field," I said.

We left the house and hunted the wood's edge toward the top of a rise. My eyes weren't hunting for squirrels anymore. I wanted to see all there was of Isaac's field. Small rock piles at the edge of the woods had been overgrown by trees. We came upon more rocks protruding from the grass as we followed the edge of the field. Looked like rock-picking was once a full-time job in that place.

I wiped my brow near the top. "Let's take a breather," I said.

I guessed Isaac's field covered ten acres, sloping off in both directions from the rise we rested on. At the apex of the clearing, near the center, was a pile of field rocks larger than any we'd passed at the wood's edge. The rock pile beckoned us to climb.

"Race ya," Mark said, taking off ahead. He had me by two horse lengths, set his gun against the heap, and climbed to the top. I stopped at the base, perplexed by the sight of such a pile of rocks. It wasn't round or oval like the shape most field rock piles take. Instead, it looked to be made with intentional protrusions, and quite tall at one time. Many rocks had fallen, hidden in the grass below.

"Bet I can jump from here," Mark said, standing on a precipice of the pile.

"Be careful you don't land on any rocks." I climbed up to the top as Mark came back around for his gun. I stood at its highest point, the pinnacle view of Isaac's field. I heard a low roar of rapids from a river nearby. Looking to the farthest edge, a glimmer of water shone through the trees. *Must be the South Branch*, I thought. I imagined Isaac cooling off at the river after picking rocks in the sweltering heat, readying the land for a family of his own. Then I became tipsy and searched for better footing,

"Hey, Mark!"

"Yeah?"

"This pile of rocks looks like a—"

Z-i-i-ing! BANG!

The distinct blast of a rifle immediately followed the whistle of a bullet over my head. I fell to my knees, then scrambled down the rocks.

"Where did that come from?!" Mark asked.

An angry man yelled from the distance, "Get off my property you good-for-nothing trespassers!" The voice came from below, near the river, only visible from the top of the rocks. "Next shot will be for keeps!" was the last we heard from him.

Mark gripped his rifle as I grabbed my rusty shovel. The two of us wasted no time running the direction we came, through the field and down the road. Neither of us slowed until we both had run out of breath.

I stopped at the side of the road with my hands on my knees, allowing blood to course like a hammer through my head. "Did you recognize that voice?!" I gasped.

"No." Mark pointed downward with his lips, letting out two full lungs of air. "Whoever it was, he's crazy!"

"That was Snuffy, I'm sure of it," I said. "Remember— the fightin' trapper?"

Mark's eyes blazed. "Is that his land?"

"I don't think so. Mr. Saddelkamp said Snuffy's a squatter, which means he's living on property he doesn't own—probably Forestry land."

"Forestry or not, I'm not going there again," Mark assured me. "I can find squirrels somewhere else."

I couldn't agree. We had hardly put distance between us and Snuffy, and I was compelled to go back—and soon. What I had seen from the top of the rock pile led me to believe that perhaps MaryAnne was right about Isaac's treasure.

I couldn't *wait* to tell her.

11

Revelation

"**Y**ou went to Isaac's field without me?!"
MaryAnne was incredulous. Her mouth hung agape as she bore into me with her bright-blue eyes. "How *could* you?"

"It was an accident, really."

"An accident!?" Wind whipped stray hairs onto MaryAnne's face. She wiped them back over the top of her head. "How do you get that far out of town—all the way to Isaac's field—and call it an accident? I thought this was *our* secret, Shoesth!"

I defended myself, "I didn't say anything to Mark—well, not really—it's still our secret."

"What do you mean, not really?"

I was at a place where more words would only land me into deeper trouble with MaryAnne. I had gone straight to her house to tell her about my discovery. We had just begun a walk down the road, and I was only able to say that Mark and I were in Isaac's field.

"I'm tired of this, MaryAnne," I said.

"Of what?"

"Of feeling like I'm in trouble all the time. Trouble with Grandma, trouble with Mrs. Krebbs—and I'm tired of being in trouble with you." MaryAnne's jaw relaxed a touch. "Can't we be friends—like we used to be?" I asked.

MaryAnne formed an inverted smile. I had missed that. Having stopped walking when MaryAnne found out where I had been, I meandered down the road again.

"Where are you going?" MaryAnne asked.

"Home, I guess."

"I'm sorry, Shoesth." Her dimples teased her cheeks. "I'll come with," she said. "I haven't held Sophie in over a week. Wait here while I go tell Mom."

MaryAnne ran back to the house while I pulled a timothy from the side of the road. There was something relaxing about the tender end of a timothy between my tongue and the roof of my mouth. It helped me think— about MaryAnne and her ways—convenient that she invited herself over to visit Sophie. MaryAnne never referred to Sophie as my sister, only as Sophie. She had made it a habit to invite herself over to visit ever since the baby was born.

MaryAnne raced back, her braids and dress trailing behind. I bit off the chewed end of my timothy, spat it on the ground, popped the grass back in my mouth, and then strolled as she caught up. MaryAnne wasted no time with silence.

"Like I said, Shoesth, I'm sorry I acted that way. I've been so disappointed since Mrs. Krebbs died, hoping you and I could solve the mystery together. But you don't believe it—and now you tell me that you brought Mark—"

I pulled the timothy out of my mouth to interrupt. "I think there's a treasure," I said.

"You believe?!"

"I said I think."

"What changed your mind?"

"A pile of rocks."

"Rocks?"

"Yes. I think the treasure is buried in Isaac's field under a big pile of rocks. You have to be there to see what I mean. We're going to solve the mystery of Isaac's treasure once and for all, MaryAnne. We just have to make a plan."

"So, when are we going?"

"It's not that easy," I said. "Have you ever heard of Snuffy?"

"No."

"He's a hermit I saw at the fur buyer's truck last spring. A mean guy. He claims Isaac's field as his own."

"Well, is it?"

"No—near as I can tell. Mr. Saddlekamp says its Forestry land, but Snuffy doesn't want anyone on it."

"Well, how do you know?" asked MaryAnne.

"He shot at me."

"What?!"

"Yup. I was standing on top of the rocks when I heard a bullet zing right over my head!"

MaryAnne gasped, her mouth agape. "Oh, Shoesth!"

"I was down off the rocks in a flash," I said. "Then I heard the guy yell at us to leave, or he'd shoot again—this time for good." I wasn't going to admit to MaryAnne that I'd never been so scared in my life. Her astonishment at my brush with death strengthened my resolve and quickened my step as we strode home. MaryAnne finally noticed the shovel in my hand.

"Why are you carrying that?"

"Thought you'd never ask," I teased with a sly grin.

"Collecting junk?" she said.

I held it in front of us as we walked, then stated boldly, "This is the shovel that Isaac Borg used to bury his treasure."

"Seriously?"

"Seriously!" I said with all confidence. "I found it in Isaac's house."

"Wow," MaryAnne breathed. "You visited his house, too? What did it look like?"

"Like a broken-down shack—no window glass, the door is on the ground. There's not much left of it—you'll see." MaryAnne took the shovel head from my hand.

After pondering it, she said, "What are we going to do, Shoesth?"

"I'm not sure yet. We have to figure a way to get back to the rocks, when Snuffy's not there."

***

I met MaryAnne at the post office the next morning at ten fifteen. She was right on time, wearing her brightest yellow.

"Did the mail come yet?" she asked.

"No," I said as I sat down on the steps. She followed suit. "Did you bring the letter?"

"Of course," said MaryAnne. She pulled the folded, worn page from the waist pocket of her dress to prove it, then slipped it back inside.

"I've been thinkin'," I said. "Our best chance of getting to the treasure is early in the morning, before Snuffy is up and about."

"And risk our lives?"

"I don't think so."

"But you said we'd have to dig under a pile of rocks. Snorty will hear us for sure."

"Snuffy," I corrected.

"Snuffy, then," MaryAnne said. "How do you know the treasure is under a bunch of rocks?"

"Because of what I saw. MaryAnne, you wouldn't believe it, because you can't see it when you're standing on the ground by this big pile of field stones. When I was on top—I lost my balance, then looked down to catch my footing—that's when I realized the rocks are piled in the shape of a huge cross!"

MaryAnne cocked her head sideways.

"That's when it hit me—MaryAnne might be right. Perhaps there is a treasure there!"

"Thank you."

"For what?" I asked.

"For thinkin' I might be right." MaryAnne's heartwarming smile was enough to break down any riff that remained, and it was enough for me to lose presence of where I was. I controlled a laugh.

"You're a goof," I said.

She didn't flinch, but wandered off in thought.

"Whatcha thinkin'?" MaryAnne didn't answer. Suddenly, she grabbed at the ruffle on the pocket of her dress. Pulling out the letter, MaryAnne opened it in a flurry and read,

"But there is hope, Alma—we've spoken of it before. Heaven is like a treasure to be sought after. I pray that you find the Truth so we may be equally yoked, and live a joyful life together—yet not by my will. I am prepared to give you all that I have; to lay it at the foot of the cross, ..."

"There it is!" she exclaimed. "*I am prepared to give you all that I have...*" MaryAnne slowed for emphasis, " *...to lay it... at the foot of the cross*! The treasure has got to be buried at the foot of Isaac's cross!" MaryAnne's excitement drove her to her feet just as the post office door swung open.

"Got some exciting news this morning?" Mr. Kingman interjected as he stepped onto the porch.

"Not really," I said.

"Just enjoying the day," chippered MaryAnne.

"All that wind last night and no sign of rain," said Mr. Kingman. "Looks like a beauty is in store."

"Full of possibilities," said MaryAnne as she squinted an eye at me. I smiled back, careful not to let Mr. Kingman see.

12

The Perfect Plan

The mail truck rumbled to a stop in front of the post office with a flat tire.

"Second one today," grumbled the mailman as he dropped a small bag on the porch for Mr. Kingman. The two of them contemplated the task before them while I signaled to MaryAnne that we should disappear. Checking the mail would have to wait.

We sat down under the brush behind the Standard Oil Station to formulate a plan.

"I've got the perfect plan," I said. "We'll go real early tomorrow, while the sun is just breaking, sneak up on the downhill side of the rocks—that's the bottom of the cross. If you're right, we can be super-quiet, and dig without moving a single stone!"

"But what if Scruffy sees us?" said MaryAnne.

"Snuffy," I said. "His name is Snuffy."

"Doesn't he have a real name?"

"How should *I* know? Anyway, it doesn't matter because we're not going to be making introductions. I'm going to bring Oscar. Oscar will let us know if there's anyone within a quarter-mile of that place."

"And if there is?"

"Then we run like the wind."

MaryAnne pursed her lips, unconvinced.

"But I don't think we'll have to," I continued. "We'll be done before the sun clears the trees. Snuffy will still be dead to the world."

"You're sounding awfully brave, Shoesth."

I liked to think so. I especially liked that MaryAnne thought I was brave. Truth was, we needed something better than what I had to pull off the treasure hunt of a lifetime.

"Here's the plan," I said. "We can't be easily seen, so dress like this." I pulled on the top of my pant leg.

"You want me to wear pantsth!?"

"No, silly! Wear something that will blend in with the woods, something the color of grass—not bright yellow, like *that*." MaryAnne considered her outfit.

"You don't like my dress?"

"Yes, I like it, I mean... that's not the point! You can't wear bright colors—including the ribbon in your hair." MaryAnne stroked the back of her braid.

"Okay. Fine," she said. "I'll wear plaid."

"Good. Now that that's settled!" I let out a deep sigh. "We're going fishing bright and early, so bring a pole." I could see I was losing her without providing an explanation. "Our parents are going to be wondering what we're doing," I said, "—and we're not going to lie. You and I are going to take our fish poles down to the creek, actually wet a worm, then continue on from there past Red Town to Isaac's field. We can't get in trouble for telling the truth, right?"

"That's only telling part of the truth, Shoesth. Besides, how is my dad going to let me go fishing with you before the sun comes up?"

"You've got to convince him. Figure something out," I said.

MaryAnne worried her brow.

"So, do you have a *better* plan?" I asked. MaryAnne pulled at the grass in front of her ruffled lace, clearing an opening in the dirt.

"I can go fishing with you at eight o'clock," she said.

"Eight!?"

"Yes, eight." MaryAnne looked up at me. "My parents won't think much of it if we go then."

"But that's risky. We'll barely have time."

Looking back down at her weeded patch, MaryAnne said timidly, "Eight."

The narrow confidence I had in my original plan had thinned to a trace. Still, after eight months of delay and doubt, after learning all we could ever hope to know about Isaac Borg, our opportunity to seize what we both believed to be true lay right at hand.

"Then it's settled," I concluded. "Eight o'clock sharp tomorrow morning at the end of the alley. You bring the letter and a fish pole—and no bright colors. I'll have Oscar and a shovel. Are you in?"

MaryAnne pulled more grass.

"Are you in?" I repeated.

Without looking up, MaryAnne said, "I'm in."

***

"Have fun at the creek!" Mom yelled as the screen door slammed on her last word.

"Wanna go fishin'?!" Oscar understood a tonal language. He knew I was going somewhere exciting when I said it like that. Besides, the fishing pole was a dead giveaway. Oscar wagged hard and reared up at the sight of my pole. He'd be by my side all day, no doubt. I grabbed a shovel out of the shed, then did a mental check on my preparations, *shovel, fishing pole, Oscar, brown shirt, dirty pants*—the perfect cover. A drop of rain tickled my face. *Even better cover,* I thought. Rain might keep Snuffy holed up.

The sight of MaryAnne already standing at the end of the alley started me into a jog. She waited there peculiarly, fishing pole in hand, and her hair out of braids. She must have been in a hurry, for MaryAnne rarely left home without braids.

"Blue?" I said in disbelief as I approached. MaryAnne glanced down.

"It's not bright. And it's plaid," she reasoned. "My other dress was dirty."

I had nothing to say to that. We started down the road toward the creek.

"Anyone wonder why you were standing in the road with a fish pole?" I asked.

"Just Mr. Saddlekamp. He said hello when he unlocked the Co-op, wondered if I was going fishing by myself. I told him I was fishing with you."

"That's all you said, right?"

"Of course. Don't you trust my judgment, Shoesth?"

I had nothing to say to that either. I walked as fast as my legs would move without running. MaryAnne intermittently ran to keep up. We were below the dam in minutes. MaryAnne fiddled with her fish pole.

"Where's the can of worms?" she asked.

I had unwound my line and held a bare hook between my fingers for MaryAnne to see, then I flipped it into the current.

"You didn't put a worm on," said MaryAnne.

"That would be a waste of a good worm."

"Shoesth! You're not being truthful."

"Fish can bite a bare hook if they want. It's up to them. Let me help you with that," I said, aggravated with watching MaryAnne try to untangle her line. "This is a mess. When's the last time you been fishin'?"

"Last summer, with you."

"Really? You don't like fishing?" I said, as I scrambled to get her line untangled.

"Not by myself."

"There," I said. "Wet your line." I spat on her hook and flipped it toward the water. "Something for the fish to go after," I explained.

"Shoesth," MaryAnne murmured and shook her head.

"All right. Let's go!" I pulled my line from the water and turned to wrap it up. That's when I saw Ricky on the bank at the edge of the road.

"Oh no!" I said. MaryAnne spied the source of my astonishment too. Ricky scampered down the hill toward us.

"There you are! Can I fish, too?!" Oscar greeted Ricky with a lick on the hand.

We looked at each other with mutual puzzlement.

"Ricky, you can't fish with us," I said. "You need to go home."

"But Mama said to come find you."

"Why?"

"We went shopping, then she said, 'go find Shoe down at the creek.'"

I could understand why Mom didn't want Ricky with her in the Co-op. He just might call Mom's attention to another "fat lady" like he did the first time he saw Mrs. Saddlekamp. But under the circumstances, I had to send him home.

"Ricky, you can't fish with us. Besides, we're not going to be here long anyway, so you can just go back home and find Mama."

"Mama said stay with you."

"Go…home…Ricky." I glared at him.

"I'm gonna tell!"

Blood pressure at my temples pained my eyes. I looked to MaryAnne. She shrugged.

Speaking through my teeth to her, I said "Should we take him?"

"I don't think it's a good idea," she said.

"If we send him home, he'll squeal on us. And if we don't leave now, who knows when we'll have another chance."

MaryAnne shrugged again.

"Listen, Ricky," I said. "We're done fishing. We're going on a long walk. You can come if you keep your mouth shut—all the way there, all the way back, and even after we get home. Do you hear?"

"Oh yeah! I'll be quiet. Where are we going?!" Ricky yelled.

I held my finger up to signal silence on his lips. Ricky stopped talking.

I took MaryAnne's pole from her, then hid both of ours in the tag alders.

"Let's go!"

13

Uncovered

We had gotten a dash past Red Town on the narrow, little-used road, when Ricky started complaining.

"Can we go back now?"

"We're not going back, Ricky. C'mon! Hurry up!"

"My legs hurt. Are we almost there?"

"Ricky, I told you, you have to stay quiet, now shush and walk faster."

Though Ricky slowed us down, we made better time than Mark and I had, hunting squirrels the whole way. A steady drizzle soaked my shoulders and the front of my legs. I had assured MaryAnne that rain was a good thing—part of our cover if we were going to have enough time to dig without discovery.

Isaac's field was in view in under an hour.

"There it is," I said, "right beyond the curve up there." I pointed with my shovel to the opening past a row of trees. I led them to Isaac's house, where we took shelter to review our plan.

"All right, here are the rules. Ricky—not a word!" Addressing MaryAnne, I said, "Speak only in whispers. When we get near the top of the rise, we'll walk in a crouch. Follow my cue. Got it?"

Both nodded. Droplets fell off MaryAnne's bangs onto her freckles. I looked her firmly in the eye.

"Now, when we get there, we'll first decide where to dig, then I'll start. We'll dig as fast as we can, trading off until we find something, or until we can't dig any further. Okay?"

"Got it, Shoesth."

"One last thing. If Oscar barks, grab the shovel and run."

"Yeah, Shoe," said Ricky.

"This is our time!" We moved quickly out the door into the rain-soaked grass, Ricky behind me and MaryAnne bringing up the rear. I kept an eye trained on each side of the field, making sure we were alone. Before long, we had neared the rise. Making long, low strides, keeping as near the grass as possible, I pressed my hand down behind me to remind MaryAnne and Ricky to lie low. I crawled the final distance to the nearest part of the stones.

"This is it," I whispered to MaryAnne. "This is the foot of Isaac's cross." We sat in the wet grass for a long minute to catch our breath.

"I'm wet," said Ricky. I glared at him, then he slapped his hand over his mouth.

"This is a big end of a cross," whispered MaryAnne. "I pictured a point, where we would know where to dig." I crawled around looking for a clue.

"Let's flatten out the grass," I said.

The three of us crawled in a semi-circle around the base of the rock pile, crushing the grass under our knees and hands. Oscar had become content with the periphery of the pile and returned to join us. He turned in a circle, round and round, making a bed for himself near the edge of our packed grass. Then he laid down in a very shallow depression just off-center of the end of the stones, out a couple of feet.

"Get up, Oscar." I pushed on his rump, but Oscar wouldn't move from his comfy bed. "Move!" I whispered loudly, and give him a smack. Oscar reluctantly stood. "MaryAnne!" I waved her over.

"What did you find?"

"Look at this shallow depression. I think it's here." Without hesitation, I stood up and jumped on the shovel, driving it deep into the sod. Tossing the dirt aside, I drove the shovel point for another bite. Again and again I dug, faster than I had worked a shovel before. Ricky and MaryAnne sat on their feet in anticipation. Ricky bounced. MaryAnne gazed, bright-eyed. I created a hole one shovel deep, a little larger than the depression, then set to digging it deeper.

Oscar's ears perked. I stopped for a moment to see what he would do. His wet nose wiggled side to side, assessing the air. Satisfied, he relaxed his ears and laid his head down on his paw.

The rain fell heavily. Dirt had become mud and stuck to every shovelful. I dug as quietly and swiftly as my arms could muster until I could dig no more.

"Here," I whispered. MaryAnne stood and took her stint at excavating the hole. "How deep did he bury it?" I wondered out loud.

"Maybe we're in the wrong spot," said MaryAnne.

"Keep digging," I urged. "We can't quit until we're sure there's nothing here." I looked on as MaryAnne managed a bit of dirt onto the tip of the shovel with each attempt. She was so light that each time she jumped on the shovel it only went half as deep as I drove it. Warm rain had soaked her dress completely through and had tightened the curls in her deep, red hair. She paused frequently to wipe her face and tuck her wet locks behind her ears.

Rested from a short break, I took over once more. MaryAnne fell to her knees and sat on her feet again, peering into the hole.

"I'm cold," whined Ricky.

"Come here," whispered MaryAnne. "I'll warm you up." Another full cut of the spade around the entire circumference of the hole, and we had dug nearly two feet deep.

"Can we go home now?" Ricky asked.

"I don't think it's here," said MaryAnne.

"Maybe not," I said. Frustrated, I jammed the shovel in the bottom of the hole to reconsider our search. It drove home with a dull thud. I looked at MaryAnne and she looked at me.

"Did you hear that?" I asked. As fast as the shovel would fly, I scraped wet soil away and flung it from the hole. Oscar got to his feet, sensing our excitement. Soon, I had removed enough dirt to expose a deep nick in the object where my shovel had struck. I wiped away as much soil as I could. Heavy raindrops washed the top of an arced wooden band, studded with rusty rivets.

"It's a barrel!" I said.

MaryAnne went head-down into the pit, digging frantically with both hands. I joined in, then Ricky suddenly showed an interest. After removing all the loose dirt, we backed out while I excavated further around the barrel's edges. Then we continued with our hands, uncovering the entire top half.

"There's a latch on it!" MaryAnne exclaimed.

I went to MaryAnne's side to help with her discovery.

"It's not a barrel," I said. "It's the top of a chest!" My pulse had reached to my fingertips. MaryAnne's breathing coursed in my ear.

We scooped deeper, exposing a padlock loop with no lock through it. Digging my nails under the latch, I pulled— but to no avail. It had rusted solid. Clouds began to break as the field grew brighter, and mysteriously quiet.

"This is so excit-i-i-ng!" squealed MaryAnne.

"Let's keep it down. We don't want to blow our cover." Holding two corners of the chest, I instructed MaryAnne, "Grab the other side. Let's see if we can pull the whole thing out. On three. One…two…three!" I heaved, MaryAnne strained. The treasure chest may just as well have been bolted to the earth. After decades of soil pressure on every side, it wasn't going to move until we dug it out to its very base.

"Never mind," I said. "I'll bust the latch open with the shovel." The shovel's blade fit securely under an edge of the rusty latch. I jumped to the other side of the hole, then pried backward. The shovel held, but nothing happened.

"C'mon! Break loose!" MaryAnne coaxed the latch.

Intent on discovering the chest's contents before being discovered ourselves, I strained on the shovel with my full weight. The handle creaked.

SNAP!

I fell backward with such force, the day went black.

14

Exposed

MaryAnne told me later that I was unconscious for a few minutes, but to her it had been an eternity.

"Shoesth! Oh, Shoesth!" A girl's voice compounded the throbbing pain in my head.

"Is he dead?"

"No, Ricky. Stop saying that!"

I blinked, ever so briefly, to painful sunlight in my eyes.

"Oh, Shoesth! You're alive!"

MaryAnne's face came into view. I felt a warm hand at the back of my head as I let my eyes fall closed again. *That's not rain*, I thought. *Those were tears streaming down MaryAnne's face. Odd*, was all I could comprehend in my haze of bewilderment. I opened my eyes once more.

"Why are you crying?" were the first words out of my mouth.

MaryAnne sniffed, then wiped away a tear. Bright crimson covered her cheek where it hadn't been before.

"You're bleeding," I said, yet unable to move.

"It's not me, Shoesth." MaryAnne held up her hand, red with fresh blood. "You hit your head on the rocks."

I rolled over onto my stomach, then brought my knees under me, keeping my face on the wet grass. I had to move if we had any hope of seizing the treasure and making an escape.

"How are you feeling?" asked MaryAnne.

Ricky answered the question for me, "O-o-o, that doesn't look too good!"

I lifted myself onto my hands and knees. A warm sensation of blood trickled behind my ear, then dripped from my chin. Grass waved before my dizzy eyes though there wasn't the slightest breeze. Still, I could feel my head clearing with each deep breath as I crawled back toward the hole.

"I guess the handle couldn't take it," I mumbled.

"It wasn't the shovel, Shoesth. The latch broke loose!"

Those words riveted my senses on the wooden chest. As fast as the pain in my head would allow, I scrambled to the lid and pried on one side with MaryAnne on the other. The old hinges resisted with a raspy groan against rust and soil, but gave way to our strength until the lid of the treasure lay open wide. The sight before my eyes was one I had only seen in a dream, from which I hoped to never wake. There lay blackened pennies by the hundreds, tarnished silver dollars, and brilliant gold coins that glimmered in the sun for the first time in 43 years. I gasped.

"Wow!" MaryAnne breathed. Her elation could no longer be contained. "Thank you, Lord, for showing us the way to Isaac's treasure! Can you believe it, Shoesth?!" she yelled.

I couldn't. I was still dazed from the stone. Finding real buried treasure had dazed me all the more. I dug my hands into the coins and let them fall back into the box, just to feel their reality and hear their jingle.

"Look at these," I said as I held out three glimmering gold quarter eagles for Ricky and MaryAnne to ogle at with me.

"What's this?" MaryAnne said, reaching in along the inside wall of the chest. She pulled out a fragile brown envelope, wet and thin from years of decay.

Suddenly, Oscar's tail rose higher than his back as he slowly moved stiff-legged toward the field's crest. A warning growl rumbled from his chest. My heart shifted from elation to flight. I slammed the treasure lid shut.

"Quick! Let's bury it!" Dirt flew faster than I had seen dirt move before, as the three of us made a feeble attempt to hide what we had exposed.

"Who's up there?" Snuffy's angry voice carried over the rise. Oscar barked viciously.

"Run!" I yelled. Before I took a second step, Snuffy lumbered forth from behind the rocks.

"Stop! Or I'll shoot!" he snarled.

We froze in our tracks. I raised my shovel and my free hand, signaling surrender. Snuffy looked just like I'd remembered. Same dirty, red hat donned his head in the heat of July that he had worn last winter. The hat didn't cover what was left of his hair—overgrown remnants that hung in oily strands. His scruffy beard matched the fury in his voice—red and ugly. Not much had changed, except— instead of lugging a pack of beaver pelts, Snuffy pointed a gun. Oscar stood outside of swinging distance. His growl was interrupted with a vicious bark every few moments while hair stood tall on the back of the dog's neck.

"Whatcha varmints doing here?" Snuffy asked, moving closer to our half-covered hole. His pungent aroma seared my nostrils as he pushed past. Nobody answered.

"Tearing up my ground, are ya? Whatcha digging fer?"

"Just playing around," I said. "No harm meant by it."

The squat, odorous hermit waddled to me face-on. Snuffy's cold gun barrel pressed against the side of my thigh as he pushed his nose up to mine. I instinctively recoiled, like the wrong side of a magnet. Chew juice darkened the corners of his mouth as he spoke.

"Well, ya done damaged my property with yer playing around!" he snarled. A drop of his spittle struck my lip as a cloud of wretched breath escaped from the cavern where a few rotted teeth remained. I nearly passed out for the second time in mere minutes.

"You're the Makinen kid, ain't ya."

"Yes, sir," I said, giving Snuffy more respect than he deserved.

"And that's yer brother?" Snuffy pointed over his shoulder with his chin at Ricky.

"Yup."

"M-m-m," he contemplated as he turned to the other two.

Looking at MaryAnne from head to toe, he said, "And who's this pretty little thang?" Snuffy reached out his gnarled fingers to stroke MaryAnne's hair. MaryAnne sucked in a deep breath while she gawked at me with eyes of terror.

"Leave her alone!" I yelled.

Oscar took advantage of the exchange, baring his teeth to the extremity of the gum. Barking with deathly ferocity, he came in low at Snuffy's leg, biting, growling, and gnashing in one continuous attack. Snuffy swung at Oscar with the barrel of this rifle.

BANG! The gun roared thunderously, tearing a furrow into the ground.

"Run!" I yelled.

We took off in a dead heat down the center of the field toward the road. Ricky set the pace, falling once along the way. We each grabbed one of his hands and pulled him along. It was time enough time for Snuffy to reload.

BANG! Another explosion rang my ears. A warning shot, I hoped. MaryAnne screamed. Oscar sped past—a sight of relief that spurred me on as fast as MaryAnne and Ricky would allow. Ricky's feet barely kissed the ground until there was plenty of road between us and Snuffy. We eased to a jog until Ricky could run no further.

"Keep walkin', Ricky," I said. "We've got to keep our distance from that guy." I instinctively kept us near the edge of the woods, ready to duck into cover at any sign of danger.

"I'm tired!" cried Ricky. We didn't stop, knowing we might still be pursued. Suddenly, Ricky fell to the side of the road.

"Ow, ow, o-o-w," cried Ricky.

I slowed to a walk and looked back. MaryAnne had already begun to retrace her steps to attend to him.

"Ricky, c'mon!" I said. We had no time for his antics. "MaryAnne, he's probably fine." I waited while MaryAnne applied her salve of sympathy. I watched her assess the situation when she reached Ricky. Then she lifted his shoe. Ricky let out a scream that should have been heard all the way to Red Town.

***

Our trip home had transformed into a dizzying journey. MaryAnne carried the shovel while I carried Ricky. That didn't last long, however. My arms gave out about the time that my ears gave out. Ricky bellered on my shoulder with every step. We had put enough distance between us and Snuffy so that I was no longer concerned about his pursuit. Instead, it was a matter of getting all of us home before my stomach gave out. Waves of nausea had been washing over me since Ricky twisted his ankle. I didn't want MaryAnne to know. We didn't need another setback. But I was beyond the point of hiding it from her much longer. I set Ricky down on the side of the road.

MaryAnne checked Ricky's foot. "It's not looking very good," she whispered to me. I examined Ricky's ankle at the shoe line. Its shade of purple had darkened to almost black. Ricky's foot didn't fit into his shoe too well anymore.

"Ricky, I'm going to take your shoe off."

"No-o-o! It hurts!" Ricky yelled.

"Yes, I know," I said. "But it will help with the swelling." I carefully pulled his lace all the way through and eased the shoe off his foot as best I could. It's a good thing we were close to the middle of nowhere and the road was rarely occupied because Ricky's screams were nigh unbearable. After coaxing the shoe off, it was clear that MaryAnne was right—it wasn't looking too good.

"Hopefully, it's just a bad sprain," I said. Oscar licked the back of my head.

"I see Oscar's concerned about you, too," said MaryAnne. "How are you feeling?"

"Sick."

"Like what?"

"Like I want to throw up." Still dizzy, I staggered to the wood's edge to expel the illness that had overtaken me. *What else could go wrong?* I thought as I wiped my mouth on my sleeve. Why was I vomiting at a time like this? I didn't understand my condition, and MaryAnne knew nothing of concussions, but I could see on her face that she was as distraught as I was ill. Feeling a bit relieved, I was ready to move on.

"Let's support Ricky between us," I said.

Each with a hand under an arm of Ricky, we struggled forth—me bearing the shovel and MaryAnne bearing a shoe.

15

Isaac's Plea

I had vomited all there was in me, and then some, before MaryAnne's dad spied us outside of Red Town.

"MaryAnne!" Mr. DuPree exclaimed on seeing the three of us. "Where in the world have you kids been?! Half of Stoney Creek is searching for you."

We didn't have a chance to answer, on account of our condition gave reason to be in a greater heap of trouble.

"Ricky! What's the matter with Ricky?"

"His ankle," said MaryAnne.

Mr. DuPree gently scooped Ricky up in his strong arms as we continued toward town.

"Shoe, we thought you and MaryAnne were fishing down at the creek. Your mother worried herself sick when it began to storm and you hadn't come home with Ri—"

Mr. DuPree stopped mid-sentence as he studied the mass of dried blood in my hair and what remained on my neck.

"M-m-m, are you a sight! You going to be okay?"

"Yeah," I muttered, keeping my head as still as I was able.

***

Mr. DuPree carried Ricky all the way into our front room and laid him on the Davenport. I flopped onto a kitchen chair and MaryAnne took up another, while the moms thanked the "guests" and politely asked them to go home. Words of admonition, elation, and scolding pounded my head. I couldn't take it in, until the din had settled and Mom was done fussing with my bandage.

"A treasure hunt," were the first words that resonated with me. MaryAnne had spoken them.

"A treasure hunt?!" snapped Mom.

"Margaret, let me handle this," said Dad. Mom spun around to check on Ricky in the front room.

"Shoe—you were on a treasure hunt, were you," stated Dad.

I closed my eyes, nodding ever so slightly.

"And what kind of treasure were you hunting for, that gave you a head injury and Ricky a bad leg?" Dad had a knack for focusing the mind when he wanted answers.

"It wasn't his fault—really, Mr. Makinen," pled MaryAnne. Her voice propped my eyes open. She glanced at her dad, then at mine. "It's the most beautiful love story. And Shoe wouldn't have gone there if it wasn't for me."

"Mary-Anne!" cried Mrs. DuPree.

"Honey, I'll handle this," said Mr. DuPree. Mrs. DuPree, visibly upset, turned to the front room where Mom had gone.

"What do you mean, a beautiful love story that the two of you went on?!" MaryAnne's dad asked. Veins popped from his neck where veins ought not to be. I searched for words while MaryAnne piped in.

"Not *our* beautiful love story," she said.

I wondered what MaryAnne meant by that. We didn't have a love story, let alone a beautiful one, and she wasn't helping our dads steer clear of the possibility.

"Show them the letter, MaryAnne," I said.

MaryAnne looked my way with a hint of trepidation. Then she slipped the worn page she had handwritten—so many months prior—from the pocket of her dress. MaryAnne unfolded the letter and held it out to her father. Mr. DuPree read silently.

"What's this?" he said when he finished. "Talk to me, MaryAnne." Then he slid the paper across the table to Dad.

MaryAnne responded timidly, "It's a copy of a letter we found in the attic last Thanksgiving."

"So Ricky wasn't the only one in Grandma's attic," said Dad, looking up from the letter.

I caught MaryAnne's eye for an awkward moment. Then she blurted, "It's about the greatest treasure and it's about a buried treasure, too!"

"You think so?" doubted Mr. DuPree.

I hadn't forgotten the coins I had taken, and reached into my pocket to gather the evidence we badly needed. Dad finished reading MaryAnne's writing.

"It's Isaac Borg," said Dad.

Mr. DuPree looked at Dad expectantly.

"Isaac Borg," Dad continued. "A suitor of Margaret's mother when she was young. The man died not long after Alek and Alma married. Some say it was lovesickness. Then there were rumors of a treasure until those false claims were finally buried and put to rest."

Mr. DuPree's charcoal brow pushed wrinkles across his entire forehead.

"Sorry, Adrien," Dad said. "Looks like Isaac's story turned into a dreamy treasure hunt for the kids."

I extended my fist over the center of the table, placing three quarter eagles to glimmer in the afternoon light. Both dads' jaws dropped in the same, stunning moment.

"Where did you get these, Shoe?!" exclaimed Dad.

Mrs. DuPree trailed Mom as the two peered into the kitchen from the front room. Mom responded to the tone of amazement in Dad's voice.

"What is going on?" Mom had apparently heard everything else, too—about Isaac Borg. "And what's all the fuss about an old flame of my mother? Did I hear that right?" Ma bore down on me. "Were the two of you snooping in Grandma's attic? Oh, there will be flames flying when she finds out. It was bad enough that Ricky nearly destroyed—" Mom halted as she riveted on three gold pieces.

"Shoe, where did you get these?" Dad repeated.

"From Isaac's treasure."

"Where?"

"In Isaac's field, south of Red Town, just beyond the hard turn—"

"Yes, I know Isaac's field. Just how did you find three gold coins there?"

"It wasn't just three coins. It's a treasure chest half-full of money," I said. "We'd have gotten the whole thing if it weren't for Snuffy."

"Snuffy's got a chest full of gold?"

I couldn't explain fast enough. And my head still hurt.

"It's not all gold," I said. "There's pennies, and silver, and some gold pieces, like these."

Mr. DuPree said, "A bunch of loot in the hands of Clem Ruskin can't come to anything good."

"He might not have it, Daddy!" said MaryAnne.

"What do you mean?"

"Well, when Oscar started growling, we closed the lid and covered it with dirt as best we could."

Mr. DuPree looked at Dad. They seemed to be communicating something to one another without saying a word.

Dad spoke first, to no one in particular. "That land isn't Snuffy's, which means the money isn't his either. It would be better to have it in trusted hands until the rightful owner can be determined. Are you with me, Adrien?"

Mr. DuPree said, "Absolutely."

"I'll hitch the wagon," said Dad. "We can be there and back before dark. Shoe, how do I find the hole that you dug?"

"Near the center of the field, at the top of the rise is a pile of rocks. It's in the shape of a cross. Stay on the road side of the rocks—that's the base of the cross, where we dug."

MaryAnne's dad appeared to be asking both of us, "Is there anything else that we should know before we leave?"

"Snuffy's got a gun," I said.

"And how can you be sure of that?"

I delayed for the right words, "Because he shot at us."

Mr. DuPree's chest fell in an enormous sigh. "I think I've heard enough on that. Anything else, then?"

"There is one thing," said MaryAnne.

"What is that?"

MaryAnne reached into her pocket and pulled out the brown envelope, then handed it to her dad.

"I found this in the treasure chest."

Mr. DuPree took the fragile paper, carefully parted the envelope and tried to remove its contents. The paper held fast to itself from years of subsoil. We all watched intently as he peeled back the face of the envelope. Barely visible on the page inside was a hand-scrawled note. Mr. DuPree read:

Praise God! My prayer has been answered, Alma— you've found the treasure. I trust that having discovered this earthly treasure, you have understood my lead—and the purpose for laying it here at the foot of the cross. And now, please tell me, Alma, have you found your heavenly Treasure in Jesus Christ? —Matthew 13:44

All my love,
Isaac

"I knew it!" MaryAnne leapt from her chair.

"Well, I never!" said Mom. "I've never heard of a man playing such silly games. Now I know why Mama didn't like Isaac Borg. Don't you agree, Lillian?" Mom looked at Mrs. DuPree with expectation. "I mean, to judge someone like that, then play hide-n-seek before he would marry? Sounds awfully childish to me!"

Mrs. DuPree took the opening to speak as Mom caught her breath. "I don't think it was childish at all," she said. "Sounds to me like Isaac wanted to win your mother's heart, but first he wanted to win her to the Lord."

Mom looked right through Mrs. DuPree. Her blank stare resonated with where I was at. The thrill of finding a real buried treasure had clashed with the oddity of how it got there. That's when MaryAnne chimed in.

"Isaac's treasure is all about the Greatest Treasure! Didn't I tell you, Shoesth? It's the most beautiful love story!"

"A beautifully bad ending," I said. I couldn't comprehend MaryAnne's repeated use of *beautiful* as a description for a failed treasure.

MaryAnne's shoulders dropped as her chin hung low.

"How can it be a beautiful love story if they never married?" I probed. "Grandma never found the treasure, she married someone else, and then Isaac died. What's so beautiful about that?"

"She might still find the Treasure," MaryAnne said solemnly.

I furrowed at her.

"Right, Daddy?" MaryAnne grasped for support. Every feature pined for a word of affirmation.

I saw no hope. The story had run its course. Treasure had been unearthed. A lifetime had passed. Hope for a happy ending to MaryAnne's beautiful love story was simply the dream of a silly girl.

MaryAnne's look of desperation glued on her father.

"You're right, MaryAnne," said her dad. "Mrs. Stenberg could still find the Treasure." Mr. DuPree grinned at Dad. Dad grinned back. They seemed to be communicating something to one another again, without saying a word.

"We'd better go while daylight is on our side."

16

Old Grandma

"You boys better be on your best behavior," warned Mom. "Grandma and Grandpa will be staying the whole weekend, and you know Grandma doesn't like a lot of commotion."

Ricky jumped off the couch and ran for the back door. No doubt his ankle had healed just fine.

Mom had spent all day cleaning house for the visit. It wasn't that Grandma and Grandpa never came to see us, it's just that they never spent a whole weekend—if they could help it, that was. I think Ricky was too much for them. It was particularly odd that they would stay more than a night with both Ricky and Sophie in the house. Neither one of them could hold silence for long.

"Why are they staying *two* nights?" I asked.

"Don't ask," Mama scolded with a nervous flurry as she ran a grey rag along the edge of the floor trim in the front room. Why Mama was makin' special preparations for relatives we saw more than once a year was beyond me. Grandma and Grandpa had been here twice last spring to see Sophie. Nothing more special about this visit was comin' to mind.

I liked it when they came, especially seeing Grandpa. He was jovial, and often quite funny. Grandma was nice to see too—in small doses. She wasn't *always* crabby, she just looked that way. Trouble was, I never knew if she was happy or if something gnawed at her insides, so it was an advantage to keep my distance.

"Do you have to dust that too?" I asked.

"Don't ask, and take your sister outside for some fresh air."

There had been a lot of things we weren't supposed to ask lately—like what happened to the treasure. Our dads recovered it without incident—that much we knew. But they weren't saying where it was. MaryAnne and I suspected that her dad stashed it somewhere for safekeeping while he located its rightful owner. She wasn't in the mood for snooping, and I had had enough trouble to last me well into seventh grade.

"Put the coins back in the box, Shoe," Dad said on the night the treasure came home. Recovering the treasure was one thing. Keeping the treasure proved to be far more difficult.

I plopped Sophie onto the cool August lawn, then sat down nearby. Sophie held one hand off the grass, balancing on both knees and the other hand. Then the first hand went down while the other went up. Normally a good crawler, Sophie wasn't going anywhere—just struggling to get both hands off the itchy turf. I laughed to myself. Not much happens at Stoney Creek when the fish aren't biting and there's no longer treasure to be found. Sometimes you have to make up your own entertainment. Sophie was usually good for a laugh, before things turned south. She didn't teeter long before her face hit the sod, as blades of grass poked into her nose. I would have to pick her up or there would be trouble from Mom.

"Oh, come here, sweetie." MaryAnne startled me from behind, then rushed to Sophie's rescue. "Shoesth, don't treat her like that!"

"Here to visit Sophie again, huh?" I said.

"And you." MaryAnne cuddled Sophie to her cheek and patted her back.

"About what?"

"Can't I just come visit?"

"There's always a reason, MaryAnne. It's either Sophie, or you've got something to tell me."

MaryAnne held Sophie's face just in front of her own and bounced her up and down. She smiled wide at the baby while talking to me.

"Well, actually there is something." She cooed and rubbed noses as I looked on expectantly. "We're supposed to talk to your grandma."

"About what?" I asked ignorantly. MaryAnne shifted her attention from Sophie to me.

"My dad said I need to confess to your grandma about the attic and the letter—and ask her forgiveness. I think that means both of us."

"You're expecting me to be there for that?"

"Dad said we're coming over Saturday for supper. He's been talking a lot with your dad about this. I don't know what they have planned, but it sounds like they want you and me there to clear the whole thing up."

"Swell."

"How do you think she'll take it?" asked MaryAnne.

"You've seen my grandma—you tell me."

"Don't say that, Shoesth. I'm not looking forward to it any more than you are. Isn't your grandma nice *sometimes*?"

"Sometimes. But you never know when sometime is."

"Your grandpa's nice. Couldn't we just confess to him?—it's his attic too!"

"It wasn't his 'beautiful love story,'" I jeered.

MaryAnne shot me a stern look—the kind that reminded me she didn't have to be gentle if she chose not to.

"We'll just say we're sorry, and that's that," I said. "It'll all blow over."

"But I need to ask forgiveness."

"Sorry, forgiveness—same thing."

"That's not true."

I had a feeling MaryAnne was fixin' to give me a semantics lesson.

"Forgiveness is bigger than sorry," she said.

I scratched in the grass for the stub of a timothy that might have survived the summer.

"Sorry is just being sad for what you did. Asking forgiveness is like getting permission to be restored with the person."

I didn't look up.

"It's a lot harder to do than sorry. But it's better, 'cause it's a word fitly spoken."

"Okay, MaryAnne, you're getting preachy on me now."

"I'm just trying to tell you the difference. Don't you want to know?"

"I think 'sorry' will be just fine for me." As I said it, a sinking feeling filled my stomach. It was the same sickening hollow sensation like when I didn't treat a girl right, and then Mom got mad at me. "Chivalry" is what Mom always said. Against that backdrop, "sorry" clanged like a misguided sword on the steel of the enemy's dark shield.

"So... what's this 'fitly spoken' thing?" I asked. MaryAnne's eyes perked clear.

"It means like a treasure put in just the perfect place."

I could see that I had opened a can of worms.

"A word fitly spoken is like apples made of pure gold. Then, they're set in a frame made of silver."

"That's weird."

"But what a treasure, Shoesth! If you give someone that—gold and silver?! That's what asking forgiveness is like."

A can of worms, it was. But on the right day, a can of worms can come in pretty handy.

***

"Ya wanna fight?" asked Grandpa. Ricky flailed aimlessly at Grandpa's waist while Grandpa rustled Ricky's hair. "All right, you little whippersnapper!" Grandpa said as he bested Ricky with two large fists.

Grandma and Grandpa had arrived just in time for sauna, except we didn't have one. Every other Finlander we knew had a sauna but they didn't live in town like we did. So Grandma and Grandpa would rough it like the rest of us townsfolk.

"Arthur," said Grandma stoically. Then she applied two pats to my shoulder. It was the most hello I could expect from Grandma, and that was all right with me. Mom and Dad gave their dutiful greetings at the back stoop before the whole lot went inside from the pending rain.

"Shoe," Dad said, "go get their overnight bag and bring it around the front room."

"Yes, sir."

Grandma and Grandpa would be taking over Mom and Dad's bed while my parents slept in the front room. It didn't happen often, but I knew the routine. I got the bag out of Grandpa's surrey as the wind cast large drops of rain at random. I took the bag in the front door and found Dad and Grandpa there, facing one another. Grandpa stood tall, his arms folded across his chest.

"Got your letter," said Grandpa. "It encouraged me all the way home from the post office."

"Adrien thinks Isaac's message will be a good opportunity to talk truth to Alma," said Dad. "Perhaps she won't shut down." I passed through the front room into the adjoining bedroom and contemplated a reason to linger, eager to hear more of what was to come.

"Can't hurt," said Grandpa. "She hasn't been open to the Word for as long as… longer than before I came to know the Lord. Thirteen years of praying…"

"We want the kids to be there," Dad said, "just Shoe and MaryAnne. It's their story as much as it is hers."

There was no answer. I emerged from the bedroom and made my way outside, leaving the two men staring at the floor.

***

Supper was a lot like supper at Grandma's with the DuPrees, except Mom was the one scurrying about the kitchen while everyone else ate. I wanted supper to last all night so the Grandma conversation wouldn't come. Such was not my luck.

The last of the dishes were being dried when the dads asked me and MaryAnne to step outside.

"Listen, kids," said Mr. DuPree. "We want to share openly with Mrs. Stenberg tonight—the attic, the treasure hunt, all of that. But we don't want to offend her."

"It's a tender piece of Grandma's history," said Dad.

"And a unique opportunity to show her God's truth," interjected Mr. DuPree.

Dad continued, "The two of you have a fence to mend with her, you know."

"Yes, I know." The sickness in my stomach wouldn't let me forget.

"She's going to be mad at us, isn't she?" said MaryAnne.

"Perhaps." Dad was solemn. "We're going to show Grandma the treasure after you've had your time to confess. It's in the shed, Adrien?"

"Yes. Under the sack, like you said."

"I want you two to bring the treasure to Grandma—but not until I give you the signal, Shoe." Dad nodded at me. I knew what he meant, and nodded in return.

Inside, Grandma and Grandpa had retired to the Davenport. Mom took up the armchair where she contained Sophie while she coached Ricky from a distance. Grandma looked spent already.

Dad brought in chairs from the kitchen. MaryAnne's mom took that as a cue and lifted Sophie out of Mom's lap, then said, "Come on, Ricky, let's go upstairs and find something to play." An awkward silence remained in the space that Mrs. DuPree vacated.

"Have a seat," said Dad. MaryAnne sat down. I sat next to her, then we were flanked by our dads—the four of us facing the Davenport. And Grandma.

"Well, isn't this cozy," Mom said nervously. Grandpa stared at the rug while Grandma barely grimaced.

"Mrs. Stenberg," Mr. DuPree started, "we wanted to talk to you about what happened at your house last Thanksgiving—to clear some things up." Grandma waved her hand without taking it off her lap.

"Oh. Alek fixed the ceiling. I'd nearly forgotten—it's all in the past."

"Well, actually, there's a little more to it than that. MaryAnne has something she would like to say to you."

I glanced out of the corner of my eye to see just how *much* MaryAnne would like to say what she had to say to Grandma. By the looks of it, she wasn't liking it at all. MaryAnne's rosy cheeks had lost their vibrant hue, and she looked like I felt—after Ricky sprained his ankle. MaryAnne swallowed real hard.

"Mrs. Stenberg, it wasn't just Ricky in your attic. Shoe and I were in there too."

Grandma didn't flinch.

MaryAnne continued, "And I got into some of your things."

Grandma's jaw tightened as her eyes steeled on MaryAnne.

"Go on, MaryAnne," said her dad.

"I just had to see your beautiful blue dress and, well... when I lifted it up, a letter came out... and I confess that I made a copy of it," MaryAnne blurted. She thrust the folded paper forth without leaving her seat. Mr. DuPree took the letter from MaryAnne and handed it to Mrs. Stenberg.

Grandma put the rumpled paper in her lap. Her chest rose while she contemplated. Then she unfolded the letter and squinted at the hand-scrawled words. She didn't read much, or she was a speed reader, 'cause Grandma looked up as fast as she had looked down to read. She glared at MaryAnne.

"I wanted to ask you," MaryAnne paused while her bottom lip quivered uncontrollably, "if you will forgive me?" Grandma's brow furrowed hard, like turned rows of soil abandoned to drought.

"Should have gotten rid of that stuff years ago!" she said, as her eyes darted to and fro, piercing through me as they passed. Then her glare halted on MaryAnne. "You had no business in my trunk, young lady."

"Yes, ma'am," MaryAnne whimpered. Her color had returned to a bright-red hue as her eyes welled up.

Grandma looked at Dad. "Are we done here now?" Grandpa placed his hand on Grandma's lap.

Dad said, "Not yet—Arthur?"

Looking for the path of least resistance, I said, "I was in your attic too. I'm sorry." The words returned to me void. Grandma breathed fast and deep.

Mr. DuPree said, "MaryAnne, tell Mrs. Stenberg what else happened." MaryAnne sat up straight for courage.

"Well, the more we found out about Isaac, the more we believed his story was true. Shoesth found the cross of stones, which meant the treasure had to be at the foot of that cross. That's when we went there to dig it up, and that's when Snuffy almost killed us!"

Mom gasped.

Mr. DuPree patted MaryAnne's knee. "Slow down, honey."

MaryAnne took a long breath, then she continued more slowly. "I copied the letter because I thought it was the most beautiful love story, and—"

"Beautiful? Vacker?! Grandma yelled. "Do you know what vacker—what beautiful is, young lady? That dreamy blue dress you got into was to be worn to the only ball this county has seen in a hundred years!" Grandma paused for breath and to gather her thoughts. Then she continued, "But three days earlier, I received this letter, written by someone who couldn't accept me for who I am, who... who was so high and mighty, he wouldn't carry through with our engagement. What makes *that* beautiful?" Grandma squeezed Grandpa's hand so hard I thought even *he* might wince.

Tears rolled down MaryAnne's cheeks in rapid succession. "It's about the Greatest Treasure," she cried. "Isaac just wanted you to know about the Greatest Treasure anyone could have." MaryAnne could hold on no longer. Her face fell into her hands and her elbows fell to her knees as she sobbed openly.

Glued to my chair, I glanced around the room. Dad nodded me the signal. MaryAnne was in no state to carry the treasure box, so Dad came with me. Out at the shed we lifted the box together. It was surprisingly heavy, being only half-full. *It's a good thing we didn't get this out of the ground and try to carry it home ourselves,* I thought. Dad stopped us at the house door.

"It's not about the treasure, you know. It's about Isaac's prayer for Grandma."

I nodded. The box we were holding had revealed more to me about what was on the inside of my dad than I had seen before. He seemed a lot more like the DuPrees than I had realized. Odd, I thought, but not unsettling.

The front room suffocated in silence. MaryAnne looked at me with wet, red eyes, sad as I'd ever seen. Dad and I set the box on the floor in front of the Davenport, then opened the lid. Grandma's eyes widened.

"What is this?" she asked.

"Isaac's treasure," said Dad.

"You're not serious!"

"Absolutely serious." Dad lifted out the torn envelope and handed it to Grandma. "Isaac left a note inside for you."

The paper shook in Grandma's wrinkled fingers as she squinted hard, slowly mouthing every word.

...and now, please tell me, Alma, have you found your heavenly Treasure in Jesus Christ?

All my love,
Isaac

Grandma turned the note over on her lap.

"I don't know what to say." Grandma's eyes raced around the room. "I..." Her hand went to her mouth. "I don't understand." Grandma sobbed tears held back for more than 40 years. I didn't know Grandma cried. I wanted to leave, but had no plausible exit. Her weeping continued for what seemed like minutes, until she gained composure to speak again.

"I thought he was playing a prank on me—an immature, young man's prank."

Grandpa gave Grandma his hanky, then wrapped his strong arm around her. As she wiped her tears, Grandma went on, "Cruel. I thought, how cruel. I had no idea he made such a sacrifice as this. Then when he died..." Grandma wept bitterly. Turning to Grandpa, she said between sobs, "He truly did want something more for me, but...what did he mean, Alek? What did he mean—'find my heavenly treasure'?"

Dad looked at Mr. DuPree then gave me and MaryAnne the nod of dismissal.

17

My First Kiss

Grandma and Grandpa still hadn't emerged from the bedroom after breakfast dishes were cleared the following morning. Clearly, Grandma wasn't doing well.

"We're going to be late for church," I said to Mom, who quietly dried dishes.

"We aren't going."

Her tone communicated "don't ask." It also told me "why?" would not be a good question. Not attending church on Sunday meant that somebody was real sick—or worse.

I found Dad outside splitting kindling in the woodshed. Odd for a Sunday.

"Good morning, Shoe." Odd for any day. Dad wasn't one for good mornings. "We're not going to church today."

"Uh-huh."

Dad split another piece of kindling. "Should be enough for Ma's cookin' tonight when we get home and for breakfast tomorrow, too."

"Home from where?"

"The DuPrees'. We're having church at the DuPrees. Asked us for lunch, too." Dad stacked the last stick of kindling on my arms. "You're looking tired, Shoe. Sleep well?"

"Not really." Truth was, my gut still churned from the night before. The sound of Grandma's weeping hadn't left me, and the DuPrees had gone home teary-eyed, every last one of them. But the uneasiness in my stomach stemmed from the "sorry" rotten can of worms I had offered Grandma.

"What's wrong with Grandma?" I asked.

"Nothing's wrong with Grandma," said Dad. "I'm thinkin' there's a lot *right* with Grandma this mornin'."

"What do you mean?"

"I mean… well, it's not for me to say," Dad said as we lingered in the shed. "We'll just have to find out, won't we?"

***

I had begun to get used to different—with MaryAnne as a friend—but I wondered what Grandma and Grandpa would think of having church in a house. It wasn't reverent.

All three of the DuPrees greeted us at their door. Faces were quite the contrast from the night before. That's how you do it for church, I thought, even if church is not a church. MaryAnne's eyes sparkled. Her braid started on both sides of her head, perfectly interwoven into one large, tapered rope that reached the entire length of her back. Perhaps being French is why it suited her so well. An oversized purple ribbon adorned the back of her head, in contrast with her freshly pressed dress. Fancy, I thought, for staying home.

"Hi," I said.

"Good morning, Shoesth." MaryAnne's lisp was hardly noticeable. Probably because I had gotten used to her saying my name that way. It was good to see her dimples on a joyful face again.

We made our way to a half-circle of chairs that had been set in the front room, facing Mrs. DuPree's china cabinet. I sat in the middle so I wouldn't have to face anyone.

Mr. DuPree started us with prayer, then said, "Let's sing 'Amazing Grace.'" Glances were exchanged as we all wondered who would lead that. Fortunately, Mrs. DuPree's perfect pitch saw us through the first two verses.

After the hymn, Grandma pulled a hanky from the sleeve of her dress and touched both eyes. She was still crying from last night, I guessed. Snooping in her attic hit Grandma harder than I could have imagined, yet something about her jaw had changed. It wasn't set as hard as the night before, and she wasn't steeling on MaryAnne, either.

Mr. DuPree stood up and talked about Saul's trip to Damascus and the bright light, and how Saul changed into

Paul. It was more like a Sunday school lesson than a sermon, so I listened for a change. There wasn't much choice, actually. I was on display, so lookin' like I was listening was all I *could* do.

MaryAnne tried to listen too. With Sophie on her lap, MaryAnne made a good show of bein' like a mama—all grown up with a baby to manage. I liked her better as a kid.

Mr. DuPree prayed again, and then we were done. Shortest church ever, which was just as well with me.

"Coffee's hot and there's coffee cake to go with it," announced Mrs. DuPree. She and Mom headed for the kitchen.

"Sounds like that's our cue," said Mr. DuPree, as he slapped Dad on the back.

I looked to MaryAnne for a cue of my own. She set Sophie on the floor, fixing to get off the chair, when Grandpa spoke up.

"So, you two have any more treasure hunts planned for the future?"

I froze. After last night, it didn't seem like the topic to resurrect in front of Grandma.

"No, not that we know of." MaryAnne shot a grin my way.

Grandma said, "I wanted to talk to the two of you."

Here we go, I thought. Grandma looked down at her hands, then back up again.

"I've got some apologizing of my own to do. What I want to say is, I had harsh words for you yesterday... and I didn't mean any harm by it." Grandma looked down as she tried to rub the wrinkles off her finger. "Thank you for finding the treasure."

I glued on my chair. Last night Grandma cried. Now she spoke kindness. Something was different, which ate at the pit of my stomach, prodding me to repair my sorry.

"Grandma, will you forgive me for getting in your attic?"

I had aged up to 13 years, and yet those were the hardest words I'd spoken. The knot in my gut melted. Grandma's face melted. Grandpa helped her stand up from her chair and then she stepped in front of me.

"Come here, Arthur," she said as she feebly held out both arms. I stood, not knowing what else to do.

Grandma gripped my arms, pulled me close, and squeezed.

"I forgive you, my boy," she whispered.

Then she kissed my forehead. The unexpected tenderness of Grandma's touch sent a rush of warmth to my toes. Her hug lasted long, as she held me tight enough to press forth tears from my eyes. I lightly touched the back of her dress as I soaked in the first hug—and my first kiss— from Grandma I could ever remember. Then I found myself astonished at the tightness in my chest, the jerking reflex of my lungs as they struggled to expel short bursts of air. I swallowed hard.

Out of nowhere I had found me a new Grandma. And for the first time in my life, I knew what it meant to be forgiven. I fell to the chair, sobbing, wondering what MaryAnne might think.

"And you, young lady," Grandma said.

I cleared my eyes enough to observe MaryAnne. She looked up expectantly at Grandma. Grandma sat down in the chair next to her.

"MaryAnne, I should have forgiven you last night when you asked, but I couldn't then. Now that I am able—of course I forgive you, too."

MaryAnne half-smiled, half-frowned, looking to hold back something of her own. Then Grandma turned in her chair slightly to MaryAnne, face-on.

"And did I tell you, I have a beautiful blue dress I've never worn—perfect for a ball." Grandma grinned. "I'm sure you would look lovely in it."

MaryAnne gasped. "Really!?"

"In due time, for the perfect occasion." Grandma smiled the biggest smile her craggy wrinkles would allow. "You helped me see something I had never seen before, MaryAnne." Grandma's voice quivered. "A truth I never *would* have seen, either, had you not *believed*."

With that, Grandma pulled MaryAnne to her side with a hug that forced one of MaryAnne's eyes shut. Good thing, too, because the other eye poured tears enough for the both of 'em.

Then Grandpa broke in. "Praise the Lord that I now bear an equal yoke with my bride." I was picturing Grandma as a bride and pondering what Grandpa meant when Mom came in the room with her coffee in hand.

"And what am I missing in here?" she said jovially.

"I just asked these two if they had any more treasure hunts up their sleeves," said Grandpa.

"Oh, I see. And what did they tell you?"

"Not that they know of!" Grandpa laughed heartily. Mom, on the other hand, saw an opportunity to ensure there would be no more treasure hunting.

"I certainly hope not," she said. "With Ricky's sprained ankle, and a head cracked open from falling on rocks," Mama looked at me. "What did you learn from all this, Shoe?"

I glanced at MaryAnne, who had dried her eyes to a sparkle. She returned the glance, expectantly.

"Never fall for a beautiful love story?" I asked, restraining a grin.

Mom pursed at me.

And MaryAnne's dimples never graced her smile more beautifully—than in that very moment.

THE END

Epilogue

The rule on the playground was "finders keepers." Not so with Isaac's treasure. His land had fallen into the hands of the federal government when his homestead failed upon Isaac's death. And so, too, the treasure. Mr. DuPree made an appeal to the curator of Isaac's treasure. That's why MaryAnne and I were each given a quarter eagle gold piece and the box to keep—both of which I've kept to this day. The trunk fell into my hands because Isaac's treasure box was too soiled for MaryAnne's liking.

Somehow, MaryAnne believed from the moment she first read Isaac's letter. Her ability to know things I could not see was a part of MaryAnne that I wish I knew. Turns out, there was a lot of MaryAnne that I didn't know.

The most wondrous experience was to witness Grandma find the Greatest Treasure—something she would keep that no one could take away. I didn't understand it. But I knew this—something changed Grandma, and just like Isaac's buried treasure—it was real.

After 43 years, Isaac's prayer had been answered:

Praying you find the Treasure.

-Shoe

Dear Reader,

I hope you enjoyed *The Suitor's Treasure* as much as I enjoyed writing it. I love to hear your feedback, so tell me what you liked, what you loved, even what you hated. I want to hear from you. You can write me at **DavidDeVowe@gmail.com.**

Also, I would like to ask you a favor. If you're so inclined, I'd really appreciate an honest review of *The Suitor's Treasure*. You, the reader, have the power to make or break a book. If you have the time, please go to my website, **DavidDeVowe.com**, and click on "Give a Book Review." It will take you to my author page on Amazon where you can select this book for your review.

Thank you so much for reading and for spending time with Shoe and his friends. I hope you will join him again as he makes a shocking discovery in *Mystery of MaryAnne*, Book III in the *Greatest Treasure* series.

In His Visible Hand,
David DeVowe

Mystery of MaryAnne

"From the very start, she was told she didn't belong in the north woods of Stoney Creek. Shoe Makinen thought he knew MaryAnne until a stranger turns Stoney Creek upside down. He discovers something shocking about her that he never would have imagined without the insight of an outsider.

Nor would have MaryAnne..."

Find all the Greatest Treasure books at

ShoeMakinen.com

Offer code: treasurebook

55825218R00085

Made in the USA
Lexington, KY
03 October 2016